DARKLING

Darkling

An erotic modern fantasy novel.

SHELLEY CASS

For my loved ones – though I
ban them from reading this.

Enjoy a free taste of the new action-romance series, 'Raze Warfare.'
A gritty urban backdrop, gang warfare, a vigilante hero, a corrupt sys-
tem, and a bisexual awakening. Join the action and enjoy the ride.

RECEIVE YOUR EXTRA RAZE WARFARE CHAPTER WHEN YOU SIGN UP FOR SHELLEY CASS' VIP LIST. GET YOUR BONUS HERE:

shelleycass.com/coming-soon-02

LINK TO YOUR FREE VIP READER GIFT

| 1 |

Lust

The fast, frenzied pace of the music seemed to quicken his own pulse so that it thudded with the beat.

Everywhere beyond his seat in the shadows there were delicious, heat filled bodies pressing together, moving to the sound as if they were animated by its power. Pushing in, rising and falling together in primal waves of dance.

One woman, scantily clad, undulated sensually on her podium at the head of the dance floor while a snake coiled around her arm, oozing its way like silk over her stomach, around her hips and about her thigh. Two more women on either side of the stage – their lips and eyelids painted black, and sharply pointed, glittering horns adorning their heads – twisted and stretched like dancing demons, driving the crowds gathered at the bases of their poles to near insanity.

A pair of bejewelled nipples pressed suggestively close to him but he waved the girl away, taking a sip of his drink and sitting back. Enjoying how the alcohol left a sharp, fresh sting in his mouth as he lowered the glass to the table.

As a rule, he did not mingle. He watched. He absorbed.

Mostly.

Yet he felt a flicker of interest, almost a stutter within himself, when a brunette walked out of the thronging crowd with her dark eyes trained on him.

She walked in her weapon-like stilettos as if she owned the world, and gazed at him as if she owned him too.

Her face was illuminated in a flash of strobe lighting and was imprinted across his mind while everything else in the club became fragmented and uninteresting. A black, cat-like mask that framed her sharp eyes only heightened her strong features further.

Dark leather hugged her chest and crisscrossed over her abdomen, while excessively short, sleek shorts showed off her long legs as she stopped in front of him and leaned in, putting her hands on the armrests of his chair.

"Mind if I have a seat?" she brought her lips close to his ear.

Then she straddled him, closing her legs in on either side of him so that he was pleasantly trapped.

"And who are you?" he asked over the music, putting his hands on her thighs.

"Don't you know?" she asked. "Aren't you shocked?"

"I'd like to know," he answered in a velvety tone. "I'm happily surprised."

She smirked. "I'm just an alley cat." The words curled from her lips, and her eyes were keen from behind the feline mask. "I noticed you. Alone and hiding in the shadows."

She pressed in, her perfume making his throat tingle.

"I work best from the shadows," he told her, reaching up to touch her lips. Red lipstick defined each sensual bow and curve, but left no trace on his fingers.

She pressed her lips to his as he gripped the bare skin not covered by the hems of her shorts and pulled her closer in his lap.

Now it wasn't the music that was sending his pulse racing, or the alcohol that made his mouth burn.

"Then in the shadows …" she panted to him, putting a hand behind his neck and kissing below his ear.

"In the shadows?" he husked.

"Then in the shadows you shall die."

As her hand moved from behind his neck to trace deeply across his throat he was surprised to feel the bite of steel.

Her blade must have been discreet and as precise as a scalpel for him not to have noticed it and for his skin not to be widely ripped open and spurting messily.

She stood and stepped out of his hold as hot blood trickled down his throat, subtly seeping into the black crispness of his shirt collar so that it was almost unnoticeable in the dark bar.

And the last thing he saw was her leaving him, taking confident, unfaltering steps through the thronging crowd. Walking away as if she owned the world, and as if he was worth nothing in it.

| 2 |

Avarice

"For God's sake!"

He felt an explosive slap sear across his cheek, his head lolling to the side.

"Come back to the land of the living!"

A second explosive slap threw his head to the other side.

"You asshole Jackson! You absolute –"

He caught a bangle covered wrist and opened one eye with a grimace.

"Charlotte," he frowned, his cheek throbbing. "It's usually more of a pleasure to wake up to you."

Charlotte glowered from where she was squatted over his blood soaked chest. "You freaking DIED in my nightclub!"

He sighed and sat up so that she had to step off him. "Yes. I distinctly remember that."

"Jackson, why did you die in my nightclub?" she asked, folding her arms and fixing him with a lethal glare.

"Well, I was murdered," he answered in a droll tone, rising from her office carpet and unbuttoning his ruined shirt.

"Also, this is more of a brothel. And, really, I should be the one laying accusations on you. Letting one of your own girls slaughter me."

"One of my girls!" Charlotte screeched. "You had my girls in hysterics! You're lucky they all owe me too many favours to go to the media!"

"I take it none of your ordinary patrons took note of my dead body then?" Jackson asked glibly.

"Of course not – but you're fortunate in that regard too," Charlotte told him sulkily. "Mick found your corpse and threw you in here before any paying customers saw."

"People are too self-absorbed these days to notice any-thing much anyway," Jackson reassured her. "It's why you and I have been feeling so sluggish. Why I came to soak up the at-mosphere of your fine establishment in the first place."

Jackson balled up his shirt and threw it at the hulking man-servant, Mick, who was filling the door frame. "Many thanks for taking care of my dead weight," he told the giant. "Now fetch me something clean and fitted."

Charlotte pouted and relented a little at last, coming for-ward and checking the healed skin at his throat. "I have been feeling sluggish," she admitted. "And you probably only reju-venated so quickly because you were surrounded in the nasti-ness of the bar. Nowhere else is so charged up."

"Gone are the war days when you could die twice in the morning and still be ready to dine by noon," Jackson agreed. He wiped at where her eyeliner had smudged and tucked a silken wave of ginger hair behind her ear.

He loved that she still styled her hair in classic, Hollywood waves after all this time.

"There's still plenty of sinning and evil," Charlotte sniffed. "But the majority of people are just suffering or numb rather than outright bad natured. It's like they have no good in them. But no real darkness either. It's putting a dampener on my energy levels."

"Hence my visit to your club," Jackson reiterated. "But we've been at this for a long while. Maybe a time's coming where there's not enough feeling out there from people at all. Maybe soon we'll just fade away."

Charlotte laughed. "You're talking about humans, Jackson Flint. There will always be enough raw, explosive human emotion to feed a darkling. Jocelyn and Edward say we'll keep going until the world breaks."

"Of course," Jackson drawled. "I taught them to think like that. Born from the first dark deeds of mankind, we'll die with their last dark deed when they destroy the world."

Charlotte ran a hand down his chest. "And in the meantime we feed off their terrible natures to postpone the inevitable."

"Feed off, or fuel?" Jackson lifted an eyebrow, peering through Charlotte's office door at the now empty gaudy nightclub beyond.

Last night there had been alcohol, narcotics, movements behind curtains, fights, passion. And over the main entrance there was a dazzling sign of lights saying 'At Charlotte's – Anything Goes'.

"Oh, tits and liquor are all in good fun," Charlotte shrugged as Mick returned with a nicely pressed shirt for Jackson. "Humans are so short lived, I might as well give them a wild ride while I feed from them."

"I support that," Jackson commented, accepting the new shirt but not adorning himself in it when Mick withdrew again. "And to pay you back for ruining your fun last night, I can help to darken the memories of all of your girls, if you wish."

"I told you, they're going to be quiet. They'd die rather than displease you anyway. And," Charlotte huffed. "It wasn't one of my girls who killed you. It must have been a random attack. In fact," Charlotte shot an accusing glare up at him then. "Sherice said you didn't deign to let any of my girls close enough to bring you pleasure or pain last night." She poked him in the chest with a manicured finger. "Maybe if you'd been with one of my girls you'd have been safely behind a curtain and out of harm's way."

"Alright Charlotte," Jackson said in placating voice. "I know your girls are fine. I just wasn't in a Sherice kind of mood."

"My girls are fine?"

"Everything about you and your girls is great," he reassured her.

"Then you still owe me for the ruined fun," Charlotte smouldered at him, leaning back against the office desk.

Jackson obediently lowered the shirt to a chair. "Yes ma'am. Anything you desire."

He lifted her to sit on the desk as her legs circled around him.

"I desire this," she said with approval, reaching down to where he leaned between her legs. "Because at Charlotte's," she went on, slowly lowering the zip of his pants. "Anything goes."

"This is why you are my very favourite darkling," Jackson answered.

And he slid the straps of her satin dress down so that it slipped to the floor.

| 3 |

Unfeeling

Jackson had almost forgotten his chilling murder by the time he finally stepped out into the world.

He smelled of Charlotte, his lips ached from Charlotte and he could still taste the last few shots they'd done together before he had hit the streets again.

He pulled on his gloves and flicked the collar of his long, thick coat up against the chill, opting to walk the back-streets to recharge himself with some inspirational, if less gourmet, low-life energy.

"Tsk-tsk," he tutted as he almost immediately felt some fingers slithering into his coat pocket. He deftly crunched those slippery digits so that there was the sound of satisfying clicks to accompany his quick feast on thief energy.

He wove through the more despicable lanes as night set in – easily snapping the arms or twisting the necks of any particularly threatening alley inhabitants who got too close to his suggestively affluent attire. The dark he absorbed from those urchins was almost tangible.

Likewise, he charitably dropped notes into the hands of those bundled up inhabitants who huddled away from him in fear or who warned him to get out of the alleys if he was lost.

The alleys were buzzing more than the streets, he thought, as he walked back out amongst the streetlights, traffic and blank faced pedestrians heading home from their mundane jobs.

Perhaps in the alleys people had to struggle so much to survive that they were more likely to be truly alive. More likely to be distinguishable as either 'good' or 'bad'.

"Alley cat …" he mused to himself, remembering red lips, stilettos and a cat mask. She'd caught his attention, and he'd allowed her to get so close, because she had been the first person sparking with genuine life that he'd come across in an age.

He felt aroused just thinking about how audaciously she'd approached and then killed him, and he found himself smiling faintly as he stopped to buy coffee at a stand. But just watching the unenthused vendor staring glumly at the whirring coffee machine was nearly enough to sap Jackson's store of dark matter again.

"Yikes," Jackson muttered. He pulled his jacket close and turned to observe the dismal sidewalk instead. But people were fixated on their phones and bumping into each other, and drivers honked their horns from the road in agitation.

"Coffee," the vendor mumbled from behind a layer of scarf, thrusting the brown paper cup over the counter.

"Mmm, delicious," Jackson winced, feeling like he'd bought a cup of the city's grit and dissatisfaction as he rejoined the monotonous lines of passer-bys.

Then he paused mid step with the cup still poised and with everyone still bustling past.

"It couldn't be," he breathed.

His 'alley cat' had just passed beneath a red neon sign across the street, and the life burning in her steps made the sidewalk seem like her catwalk while everyone else became part of a faceless audience.

She zipped her closely fitted leather jacket up to her chin and pulled shoulder length, glossy hair into a low ponytail as she walked.

"Oh boy oh boy," he whistled between his teeth.

She strode towards a shiny black motorcycle, donning a helmet and revving the bike to life.

He focused intently, listening beyond the noises of traffic and pedestrians for sounds of chaos or death coming from any of the shops across the street. But there were no screams, cries, or gurgles for air in any of the buildings. So perhaps she had not been on a kill job, or perhaps she had been subtle again.

"Be still my darkling heart," he smiled to himself, ditching his cup of dissatisfaction and at once allowing his physical body to turn to smoke.

He quickly blurred along the road after her like a rogue wisp of shadow.

Or in this era – like a puff of exhaust or factory smog.

| 4 |

Enigma

In his shadow form Jackson followed the trail of sound left by her motorbike, speeding his way between endless streams of traffic, just as she must have moments before.

He re-materialised where the trail ended at a flashy four story apartment block. It was just outside the heart of the city where the streets were glitzy but quieter, and he closed his eyes to see better.

He used his mind's eye to pick up on any ripples of residual energy – a shadow trace left behind by any living or technological thing. Whirrings and movements always created a sort of imprint in the atmosphere of what had passed moments before.

"Yes, baby," he breathed as he saw a misty image of a large roller door drawing upward – the entrance to the parking lot that made up the lowest level of the building. She'd thundered in to park next to an entire row of different bike and car models, with some looking like they had been purchased purely for pleasure, and others for discreet business.

The roller door was closed now in real time, but he was able to stretch his vision to catch sight of how she'd crossed to an elevator and pressed the button for the fourth floor.

"Gotcha, kitty cat," he grinned, stooping down and then launching up into the air, catching himself at the second story with a grip on a ledge, then propelling upwards to land on the ledge of the fourth floor.

He started at first when he peered at the glass and found his own beautifully dressed reflection staring fixedly back, but then quickly assumed his shadow form once more so that even he could hardly see himself.

Then he noticed her, already walking through her lofty apartment in just a tank top and underwear, draining a bottle of water and holding a case of some kind. The whole vision was like a scene out of a film; the roof to floor walls of windows creating a cinematic, screen-like image.

"Somebody get me the popcorn," Jackson whispered.

She crossed her kitchen, and he noticed that there was a gash running across the top of her leg.

She swung herself up to sit on a black marble benchtop and cracked open the case she'd been holding.

When she withdrew a lighter Jackson prepared himself to accept that she had a vice for both cigarettes and murder, but instead she continued to also withdraw a thick sewing needle, sterilising it with a flick that brought the flame to life before she deftly threaded the needle and began stitching. She didn't grimace as she pulled the edges of her skin back together.

"Woah," Jackson blinked, taken aback.

She snipped the thread free and lifted a phone, holding it

between her ear and shoulder so she could sift through some bandages.

Jackson quickly strained to hear through the pores of the thick glass.

"Yes. Alley Cat checking in," she was saying. "Of course. Job done. Helen was feisty, but I got her."

Helen … Jackson mused to himself. Could that have been politician and human trafficker Helen from the inner city? What had gone on there?

Alley Cat ripped a dressing from its pack and pressed it against her leg as Jackson's eyes narrowed at the brand of adhesive.

"It's fine," she said. "I'm doing an overnight healing, courtesy of CARE's best products."

As someone who made friends with the most powerful people in the world – all who had the most up to date things and who had the most corrupt vibes to recharge even the weakest darkling's soul – Jackson had never heard of 'CARE', or of a particular type of dressing that could stimulate healing overnight. It would be a surgeon's dream invention. But perhaps it had never fetched an offer hefty enough to tempt its designers to share the lifesaving development with broader society.

"I dislike local jobs," she said in a blunt tone. "They draw attention to my area. Now that the people-mover-politician and CARE's kingpin are down, I'll only do a local job again for someone big." She hung up and slid back down from the bench.

She put her full weight on both legs and strode easily through the apartment, switching off lights.

When Jackson heard a shower begin to run he turned to sit with his back against the cold, hard window, his eyebrows raised.

"Who are you?" he let the question issue out into the air.

But the only answer was the ongoing sound of running water from inside.

| 5 |

Fixation

His murderess was fascinating, and Jackson had forgiven her completely. By his second week of observing her, he'd even come to hold her in the highest regard.

She had such great standards. Such skills. Such intrigue.

She made contact with no one but the mysterious phone caller, and Jackson still only knew her by the call sign Alley Cat. But he had come to be almost intimately familiar with her movements, and had become so enthralled by her that he'd hardly felt the urge to even return to his own luxurious manor for more than a change of clothes.

It was centuries since he'd felt so alive – it beat the feeling of a fix from even the worst politician's dark soul on a lonely night. And following her exploits had become a form of thrilling entertainment for Jackson – a sort of game as he tried earnestly to puzzle out how each of her beautifully atrocious actions connected.

Adding to the allure was the fact that following her exploits had been no simple feat.

For instance, in the first week she had travelled to Russia to assassinate some business moguls he'd known for decades. Their demise did not trouble him, and nor did the fact that she seemed to be whittling away at his collection of darkling fuel. Jackson was instead challenged by her speed, for by the time Jackson had followed her traces, all he'd found was a bullet that had been fired at shockingly close range into mogul one's forehead, and mogul two's body left slumped over and floating in a massive fish tank.

Alley Cat had already moved on, and though the bodies were still warm, Jackson had been left trudging through the snow for hours, following blurred glimpses of her residual shadow to a train station – where he had finally managed to find out she'd headed to Germany.

He'd been unable to find her again until she'd popped up in China. He'd made it just in time to witness her precise execution of a drug lord he'd had the pleasure of sapping darkness from only recently. She'd used a silk scarf and a deadly, but decorative knot that had so neatly, so deftly strangled her target, that Jackson himself had been left breathless by the vision of her artful slaughter.

However, there was something about the murderess herself that was not dark enough to fuel him as he ghosted along after her, so he'd had to part from her in Australia to find a juicy suburban rapist to drain before he could go on. And that was when he'd lost her completely.

He had been a regular storm cloud of swirling, moody shadow as he'd made his way back across the seas to find his own home.

To keep from brooding by his fireplace he'd gone to Charlotte's, where he'd had to act like he was in a Sherice mood. But sparkly fingernails, eye shadow and nipple jewels aside, instead of being enthralled by Sherice's heavenly charms he'd been distracted by memories of Alley Cat in the very same club.

To keep from huffing and moping about the streets he'd gone on an arson spree of drug lord houses across America. But crackling wood, blistering skin and exploding labs hadn't truly enthralled him.

To perk up his darkling spirits he'd even dropped some corrupt cops from sky scrapers throughout Britain. But the thrill of slowly letting their hands slip from his, their own weight dragging them down, was ruined when all he could think about was the tragedy of him losing his own killer.

| 6 |

Unknown

"She killed you too!" Jackson crowed. "She's back in town!"

By chance he had stumbled across his fellow darkling, Edward Scott, in an alleyway and he was now hauling Edward's limp body through the backstreets. The traces of her lingering presence around Edward were tantalising.

"Lucky she took another local job. I'd given up checking her apartment!"

Edward was not yet responsive, but Jackson was jubilant to have found another darkling with a slit throat. It brought back fond memories of his own first encounter with Alley Cat.

"What was 'big' enough about you for Alley Cat to take you out?" Jackson asked his dead friend. He'd never been able to figure out why she had gone after himself originally, or any of her other victims.

Taking a better hold of Edward's bloodied designer shirt, Jackson excitedly surrounded them both in his shadow form and blurred them back to his manor.

"Hell's bells," Edward murmured thickly as Jackson slid him across gleaming marble floors towards the fireplace of the main hall.

"Tell me all about your murder," Jackson demanded keenly. "Was it exhilarating?"

"Jackson Flint?" Edward moaned slowly. "What is wrong with you? This is why I don't visit."

"Why are you here then?" Jackson patiently let some of the darkness of his own spirit ebb out to settle over Edward, aiding his friend's healing process.

"Business. Seeing you is hardly a pleasure." Edward's flawless, dark features contorted with a grimace as he sat up.

"You adore me," Jackson countered, leaning in to unbutton his friend's bloodied shirt before fading out to a pristine bathroom for a wetted cloth and reappearing with it. "Who else provides you with such care when you've been resurrected?"

Edward grunted, but let Jackson sponge at his throat and chest.

"You haven't brought me back to life since our mercenary days in Europe," Edward told him, tilting his strong chin back.

"But I kept you entertained throughout our times with the Mongols and Vikings," Jackson reasoned, throwing an arm around Edward's dark, smoothly muscled shoulders. "And I'm much easier to be reborn with than Charlotte."

"Life with Charlotte," Edward winced, but then smiled. Jackson was now tracing the wet cloth over Edward's chocolatey collar bones. "I've loved her whorehouses across the centuries. And you loved her regularly enough that she stayed out of my hair," Edward ran a hand over his closely shaven head.

"I loved you both regularly enough to keep everyone happy," Jackson countered – gripping under Edward's arms and lifting him up. "Jocelyn too, whenever you've been a pair."

"True," Edward sucked in a breath, allowing Jackson to deposit him in an armchair. "Though happy is not an easily achieved state anymore."

"I've been saying the very same, my friend." Jackson crossed to his liquor collection and poured two glasses of bourbon before handing one over to Edward. Yet he couldn't help but reflect on how much his fascination with Alley Cat had recently revived his spirit.

"People are downright empty." Edward closed his brown eyes as the heat of the alcohol touched his tongue. "So vacant. It's disturbing."

Jackson seated himself across from his friend, crossing one leg over the other. "But we still manage to get sustenance."

"Sustenance isn't the problem," Edward warned. "It's that sucking the darkness out of people isn't making them any better anymore. Mark my words, soon everyone will be dead inside. Even the worst people don't feel enough passion in this time."

"Is that why you've resorted to business once again?" Jackson asked, swilling his glass and observing Edward's business-like, bloodied trousers and unbuttoned shirt. "Surely our prospecting jaunts throughout the ages have left you wealthy enough for a few more lifetimes."

Edward was quiet for a moment. "Boredom, restlessness

and hunger drove me to look for something more." He rotated his glass in his hands, eyes down. "For a cause."

Jackson watched his friend's face in the wavering light from the grand fireplace.

"Was it this cause that got you killed? And," he lifted an eyebrow. "Was it a beautiful assassin who killed you?"

"Very beautiful." Edward appeared mildly uncomfortable. "And yes, it is likely that it was the cause that got me killed. In fact," he sighed. "That's why I came. I wanted your advice about the things I'm involved in. And I was worried that these things might get you and Charlotte killed too. Among others of our kind."

Jackson's eyes narrowed then. "I was killed not long ago in Charlotte's Bar. Perhaps you should explain."

"Now don't be hasty to react." Despite Edward's great size, he swallowed nervously as he regarded his more slightly built companion. "You shift from devilishly seductive, to fiendishly jovial, to gravely serious much too quickly."

"Explain." Jackson remained poised in his chair, but his expression had become wintry.

Edward ran a hand over his scalp again. "Some months ago I was approached," he said.

"Approached," Jackson let the word evolve in his mouth slowly. "By humans?"

"Jackson, they knew everything about me – about us all – already," Edward answered quickly. "They are part of such an advanced scientific corporation that they practically run the world without most of the population even knowing it. Not even we have realised it, we who have known this world so well."

"So they must have seemed the perfect corporation to become involved with. To spill our secrets to." Jackson carefully set his glass down and uncrossed his leg.

"I told you, they already knew us," Edward explained emphatically. "And they did not force me to communicate with them. They invited me into their headquarters."

"So you confirmed their suspicions about us. You accepted their cordial invitation. Simply because they did not abduct you?" Jackson stood and circled to stand behind Edward's chair, placing his hands on Edward's shoulders. "Next you'll be telling me you went to their high tech labs and let them examine you. You'll be telling me that, skin cell by skin cell and blood sample by blood sample, you let our mysteries be known by mortals."

Edward was quiet and Jackson put a hand on the back of Edward's neck now, giving it a firm squeeze.

"Jackson Flint, believe me. I only did it because they can help us. And the world. This group is big. They call themselves CARE, and they run everything. If they are to know about us anyway, it is best that they are allies." Edward reached to pull Jackson's hand down to his exposed chest. "My heart is still darkling, I have not betrayed us."

Leaning over him, Jackson spoke beside Edward's ear now, so that Edward could feel the warmth of Jackson's breath. "You'd best tell me everything they learned from you, and everything they want."

Edward shuddered.

"Their doctors were from every continent," the darkling answered earnestly. "Their technology was incredibly advanced, and they had offices for liaisons of all kinds. According to the plaques above the labyrinth of doors they have liaisons for media and advertising. Liaisons for food production, clothing and technology brands. Liaisons for construction, for film production, for medicine, for education, for intelligence collection, even for world leaders."

"So … they communicate with, or own, parts of every major feature of society?" Jackson's arm wrapped firmly around Edward's chest like a seatbelt now, but it was more of a support than entrapment. He was listening.

"They explained that they had worked out exactly what I was and where I lived by following a trail of metadata. They have technology that can pick up on patterns and present analysis of these. The patterns they picked up on came from coded communication from my own self, as well as accidental or unintentional references other people made to their moods throughout texts or posts or chats, which then appeared to match my whereabouts. It seems that these slight connections were enough to set off alerts and spark their interest, and they were able to track deeply enough to find and study me."

"Did they run tests?" Jackson's voice remained close and soft.

"They did not need to," Edward answered. "By the time they approached me, they had enough footage of my activities, both in my tangible and shadow form, to have all but a word to define me. They also knew enough about the patterns to have found countless others of our kind."

Edward felt Jackson's arm tighten around him in a slightly more constricting embrace, pushing for a true answer.

"Though ... I did allow them to take a sample of my blood and tissue."

Jackson scowled and Edward could sense it when Jackson spoke next.

"What conclusions did they reach? They cannot have been good if they sent an assassin out for me, and for you, their great helper."

"It can't have been CARE that sent the murderess after us," Edward answered, turning his head slightly to peer up at Jackson. "If anything, they would be doing all they can to get me to come back to them – I left secretly to come to you. To tell you what was happening. Because CARE want us to help them. They believe we should reveal ourselves, and become a kind of dark police force, actively absorbing the darkness from society."

"Is that not what we already do?" Jackson's eyes held Edward's upward gaze. "We are darklings. We take the darkness from people to fuel ourselves, but we do it from the shadows. We do not step out into the light to be seen or feared or interrupted. And we certainly do not need overseers such as this 'CARE'."

"But they could pinpoint our targets," Edward said with an appeal in his voice. "We would be able to actively target darkness that has grown to dominate the globe, and to eliminate darkness before it could truly taint a soul. We would be able to shift how the world functions. Maybe people would have a chance to become better, livelier again, if they exist in a different system."

"And what," Jackson purred in a low voice, "would happen to us if there was eventually no darkness left to feed upon?"

Edward swallowed hard.

"What would CARE gain?" Jackson went on slowly. "And why is a murderess working against such a large corporation … when the risk must be so great?"

"I do not know," Edward admitted breathily. "But I think working with CARE could lead to a brighter future for us shadow beings, and for everyone. The murderess must be confronted."

Jackson leaned in closer still, and pressed his lips to Edward's. Then he stepped back from the armchair.

"It is my right," Jackson told Edward, smoothing his dark hair back. "She was my murderess first, and it is you who drew her attention to me."

"Of course," Edward replied respectfully. "Though it may be out of our hands who confronts her first. She stole my phone, which was a gift from CARE that they might trace."

Jackson became grim. "She only stole my life, nothing else was missing."

Edward shook his head. "Perhaps she has stolen your blood and tissue, in contrast to the free will that CARE granted me."

"So your new employer wants their research, wants a police force and wants Alley Cat stopped," Jackson remarked. "We'll see."

"What do you mean to do?" Edward asked.

"I mean to find out what is truly going on," Jackson answered coolly. "I recommend that you make yourself scarce and cut your foolish ties with mortal corporations until I say otherwise. Are we clear?"

"Yes friend," Edward complied.

Jackson turned to leave, straightening his cufflinks and collar. "Next time I hope to have a moment to actually appreciate having you half dressed in my vicinity."

"Yes friend," Edward smiled a little this time.

Then Jackson's features blurred, darkened and faded to shadow.

| 7 |

Toxic

Jackson was dangling his legs over her fourth story ledge, moodily considering what Edward had revealed, and what it could all mean when her bike came tearing down the street.

He tensed in surprise and leaned over the ledge when she angled the bike to skid under the rolling garage door even before it had fully opened. He heard the bike spark and grind to a stop, the roar of its engine being cut off, and he quickly closed his eyes to find the immediate traces of her abandoning the bike inside, slumping in the elevator up to her apartment, and then staggering out into her own main room.

He quickly went shadow and opened his eyes to see her half collapsing on the reflective, black bench top as she hastily grabbed for the medical case he'd seen her use previously. The one that had had 'CARE' products in it, he remembered.

One shaking hand gripped the bench while her other unclasped the case, hurriedly searching until she'd seized a little green glass bottle.

But her hand slipped from its grip on the bench and she

folded in on herself in pain, dropping down as she lost consciousness.

"This won't do," Jackson hissed, and though it was a strain, he began to press his shadow form against the thick window glass – and then into it.

This was not a nice thing to do, as his entire shadow being abruptly became more solid and connected to the grainy glass instead of shadows or physical body. He felt stretched, he felt shiny, he felt much too inanimate, but because he could see where he was going his mind kept hold of a need to move forward through the pores of the glass instead of a need to conform and become stuck.

He finally seeped his way free, nose tip and toes surfacing to become whole again while the rest of him followed after.

Even as Jackson solidified he took quick strides across the room to stoop over Alley Cat, finding her pale, with eyes closed and breathing quickly. There was a shallow slice that ran across her breast bone and as he plucked the small green bottle up from where she'd dropped it he drew his breath in at the sight of the label.

"CARE's Ultimate Antidote – a dose for any poison?" he asked her prone form, and quickly pulled her leather jacket further back from her shoulder so that he could examine the gash. "And you're hotter than ever," he mused, feeling the heat almost steaming from her skin.

Jackson smoothly unscrewed the bottle's lid and tilted her head back, holding her jaw so that her lips parted and he could drip the small dose between them. When the bottle was near empty he stripped her jacket off completely and grabbed a damp cloth from her bench, scrubbing at the cut before drizzling the last drops over the wound itself.

Running his hands over the rest of her body, purely to check she was otherwise in one piece, he became convinced that she was not harmed in any other way. So he scooped her up and went in search of her bedroom.

"Don't feel obligated to reply," he commented thoughtfully. "But your apartment is a little sparse." He discovered her large, neat bed and placed her dutifully on it.

"I hope it's not a reflection on you, my dear," he went on as he took his time unlacing her boots and then draping the bed's cover over her. "All sleek on the outside and empty on the inside. That would be disappointing."

Curious, he held his hand out over her sleeping form and closed his eyes so that he could see better. "Despite how we first met, I don't see enough shadows for you to make good darkling food," he told her clinically. "Instead," he frowned. "You're a rather neutral colour inside. A mix of the right amount of shadow and light. Which is not the expected shade for a murderess."

Alley Cat did not stir with interest or enthusiasm when Jackson opened his eyes to peer at her again, so he resolved to explore her apartment for answers to the puzzle she presented.

Adjoining the bedroom he found a meticulously kept bathroom of luxuriously shiny surfaces. The kitchen was equally as ordered with a well-stocked fridge of wholesome foods and drawers filled with carefully folded, single toned dishcloths and nice rows of utensils.

He fished in her discarded jacket pocket for her phone –

Edward's was not there – and he intently held his fingertips over the screen until he could sense her traces of frequent energy and follow them to unlock it. Yet the device yielded little information, as it had been set up to automatically and irrevocably delete all call, search, location and message history.

"Not even a high scoring game to tell me how you pass your non-murderous hours," Jackson sighed as he passed on into the main area, which was bare of photographs and magazines, and was even missing a sound system that could have enlightened him about her music tastes.

"You seem military," Jackson deliberated, running a finger across a black, reflective shelf. Only one modern ornamental sculpture filled its space. "Or were you a house keeper in another life?"

In frustration he closed his eyes once more and searched for past, faint traces of her movements, and though he was hardly able to make out her image he could vaguely register her using the wide room for exercise.

"Surely there's more to you," he insisted, tapping the toe of his dress shoe on the dark, gleaming floor boards as he mentally scanned the rest of the simplistic room and found nothing.

He focused harder as he noticed that her energy seemed to make an almost imperceptible line toward him too, and he wondered why she might often come to stand in his exact spot.

He opened his eyes to examine the very ordinary corner of the room, running his hands over the cement rendered walls nearest him. "Not much you can do with cement," he muttered, and instead knelt down to inspect the floor boards.

"Very interesting," Jackson breathed, at last noticing an almost imperceptibly raised 'nail head' protruding slightly from one of the boards closest to the wall. He reached out to straighten the angled nail, and at once a square of the floor boards lowered with a hiss and slid away like an automatic trap door.

"Well that's better," Jackson raised his eyebrows, peering into the dark opening in the floor. He discarded his heavy over coat and unbuttoned his shirt cuffs, expertly rolling them up before lowering himself into the dark space below.

| 8 |

Secrets

It would have been too dark for anyone but a shadow born darkling to be able to see unaided, but Jackson was gleeful to find himself in a hollowed out space between Alley Cat's floor and the ceiling of the apartment below.

There was only enough room to half crawl and half slither along a trail that had been cleared, and it would probably sound like some awful creature was moving through the ceiling of the apartment below, but Jackson keenly inched his way further in.

It did not bother him that his shirt buttons would be getting scratched or that the fine material of his trousers would be fraying, for he'd just discovered where all the interesting items that had been missing from the dwelling above had been stowed.

"A priceless French Madonna icon," Jackson surmised in surprise as he regarded a sixteenth century statuette. "And ... is that an English tapestry? Twelfth century, give or take." He chuckled to himself, tracing his fingers over a hand mirror that could have come from the Titanic itself. He didn't doubt the authenticity of any of the items. "She's a murdering thief?"

Crawling onward he found a fragile parchment that could have been a map to find treasure beyond his wildest dreams, but he was more interested by a number of large hard cover cases under the paper. Inside the cases were a wide range of weapons, some subtle and some barbaric, as well as more medical equipment and explorer type gear.

But on the cases themselves was another logo that read 'CARE'.

"Tut tut," Jackson said softly. "Perhaps Edward was wrong."

Dusk had descended and the apartment was in shadows when Jackson at last levered himself up and out of the floor, pulling himself back from the gaping opening.

"I hope you enjoyed yourself," a dangerous voice purred. And he felt Alley Cat's blade press against his throat in an almost familiar way.

He shivered with a smile and reached over his shoulder impossibly quickly, seizing her wrist. In an unnaturally deft, acrobatic move he pulled her forward and over, into his lap, where he held her knife wielding hand to her own throat.

"What a reception. I broke in here and saved you," Jackson grinned.

"And yet I thought I'd killed you," Alley Cat simmered, a little out of breath. Circles of heat stood out against her pale cheeks, and her skin was glistening with a light sheen of sweat as the toxins left her body.

"Yes," Jackson agreed. "You did it very efficiently. It's not your fault I'm alive. But working for CARE, you must know all about that."

Her lips curled in a snarl and her eyes flashed dangerously. "You've got to be joking. You, accusing me of working for CARE. You still don't recognise me."

"No," Jackson went on. "But I saw the brandings on some of your treasures." He moved the knife away from her skin. "And it's no matter. Fortune smiles upon you, for you've got me intrigued. And I won't hold my death or your job against you – just yet."

"You must've hit your head. But fortune smiles upon you, for now you'll become one of my treasures," Alley Cat replied silkily. "Until I know how to kill you again properly."

Jackson immediately became enamoured by the idea of even just temporarily becoming one of her treasures, and made to lift her. But he was not expecting her sudden flare of energy.

The moment he had half straightened she swivelled around his body, swept his legs out from under him, and sent him toppling down through the opening in the polished wooden floor again.

She had the opening sealed in moments, and Jackson found himself ensconced in the claustrophobic, secret space once more.

He puffed indignantly up at the dark slats over his nose, unused to being surprised or winded. Yet before he could even compose a snarky comment, he heard her suddenly hissing a breath of annoyance above him.

Then he heard the cracking sound of her door being broken in.

There were quick, heavy footsteps – enough to suggest six or so unwelcome guests entering Alley Cat's dwelling. And there was the faintest sound of her stepping into a battle stance.

"Unacceptable," Jackson glowered. She was his. Even if he was currently her trapped treasure.

He sensed more than heard her rushing at the newcomers, felling one immediately, and he strained to ignore the image traces lighting up the room above as she danced around them with her knife.

He had to focus on not just going shadow – but on oozing his way up through the thin cracks between the floorboards.

This was not as simple as passing through glass to a clearly visible other side. This was intricate, this was tense, this was the difference between him rising up in a heroic haze, or ending up as grout between floorboards for eternity.

But the wisp of darkness that he had become paused and swore when he heard the solid, meaty sound of a fist hitting flesh while Alley Cat grunted in pain.

Despite the miracle antidote concoction, she had been in dire straits just an hour or so earlier, and she was not yet back at full, murderous capacity.

Grunting darkly, Jackson shimmied his mist out from between the cracks, issuing up from the floor like a genie and taking shape from his torso up, not bothering to wait for solid legs.

He was faintly surprised to see the mask of shock Alley Cat was directing toward his heroic haziness, even though the man she had just stabbed through the heart had himself clearly been a very unnatural person.

"Mister White?" a confused voice addressed Jackson then. "Why are you here?"

"Mister what?" Jackson muttered, turning and taking in the sight of five other male and female intruders, who each had totally dark eyes. As if the light had been sucked right out of them and there was no white left.

But then one of the grim intruders lunged at Alley Cat, and Jackson was launching forward. He went shadow, right through the attacker, and the woman dropped as he sucked up her darkness.

He hardly had time to reflect on how he had in fact never sampled so much darkness from one being, before he felt the woman die and he solidified again on the other side of the room, suddenly energised far beyond what was normal.

"They don't usually die unless I mean them to," he speculated for Alley Cat's benefit, hiccupping a little as he dabbed at the corners of his mouth. "But I feel quite full. As if almost all she was made up of was darkness."

Surely that was impossible. No human being could be completely without light.

"That's not Mister White!" the next void-eyed crony cried out, and he launched now at Jackson.

"Who the hell is Mister White?" Jackson frowned at the man, who was mid-launch.

But Jackson Flint was no glutton, and he felt almost drunk off the one woman he'd already faced. So he simply let his hand turn to shadow and plunged it into this new opponent, solidifying his fist around the man's heart.

One squeeze and the opponent was gone without Jackson

trying to drink anything in. Yet, still, just that contact with the man boosted Jackson's adrenaline further.

Jackson cracked the skull of the next woman the old fashioned way, bloodying his knuckles, and then seized the last man by the gullet.

Jackson turned both his hand and his victim to shadow as the man gurgled a scream. Dramatically energised, Jackson was able to easily thrust the now intangible man through the closed window to dangle outside.

Jackson didn't release his grip on his kicking victim, but he did glance back around the apartment to find it now empty. And then there was the faraway roar of a motorbike being kick started down in the garage.

He had meant to question the man, but Jackson's tension got the better of him as Alley Cat suddenly burst into view on the street below – just a streak of black as she raced away like a wasp.

Jackson sighed, forcing the now lifeless man to remain shadow permanently – drawing his hand back in when his victim had faded to nothing.

He examined and then turned each of the other corpses to shadow too, so that it was as if they had never existed. But his mind was on Alley Cat.

She had been disgruntled to find Jackson alive, and had been quite surprised to see Jackson's shady nature and abilities on display.

Perhaps her employer had not told her everything about her assignments, he mused, using a pristine dish cloth to polish the blood from his knuckles.

All the same, he did not pursue her in order to darken her

memory. He did not want her to forget, and seeing as she would not be coming back to her apartment any time soon, he would need her to be the one to come to him.

In the meantime, he was stuck on an oddly soaring high.

He would have to let off some dark, dark steam.

| 9 |

Energised

"Jax, what happ –" Edward gasped as Jackson materialised behind him, a sudden apparition in the bathroom mirror.

"I am in no mood to talk," Jackson growled, ripping Edward backward and into his arms. "You're in my favourite shirt."

He pressed Edward's back against himself, breathing in the scent of brandy and borrowed cologne before reaching around to rip that favourite shirt open, sending buttons flying.

"You're drunk on power," Edward uttered. "How many people did you drain?"

Then he moaned as Jackson roughly ran his hand down a chocolate chest, and ran his teeth over a chocolate neck. Greedily, he ran his hand down further to put pressure on the stiffness already straining against Edward's trousers.

"Shut. Up," Jackson grinned evilly, reaching around to tug at Edward's belt.

But repeatedly pushing Edward up against a cool marble

wall only further enlivened the dark energy coursing inside Jackson, making him hungrier.

"He's manic," Charlotte said, wide-eyed when Edward brought Jackson into her office. "Since when does Jackson Flint want an orgy before sun down?"

"Since ... I drained ... an almost wholly corrupted human," Jackson groaned, dragging Charlotte closer by her wrist.

"How is that possible?" Edward asked over Charlotte's giggle. "No human is all bad. And we've all remarked on what a drought of true energy there has been."

"Don't know," Jackson's pants were off now and he tore Charlotte's underwear, hoisted up her skirt, and lifted her leg so that it circled his waist. "But ... if I'd gorged on ... any of the others who were with her, I think I would have ... literally exploded," he said between thrusts.

"There were more of these unnatural people?" Edward frowned. "We must be careful. Unwittingly leeching from them could really kill us, if just one person did this to you."

"You're so full you're buzzing, Jackson. Giving me goosebumps," Charlotte panted when Jackson released her now swollen lips.

"I'm so overcharged it hurts," Jackson shuddered, his skin thrumming with static. "I have to get this energy out."

Charlotte wrapped both legs around him so that he was holding her up. "Well I'm here for you," she husked gleefully, and he bit into her shoulder tensely.

"Perhaps we should ask the people at CARE what they know of these dangerous new beings," Edward suggested uneasily. "They know of us, maybe they know of other unnatural happenings."

"A human group knows about us?" Charlotte cried out, this time in alarm rather than ecstasy.

"Edward," Jackson glowered. "Either add to her pleasure or avoid hindering it."

"They might be able to protect us," Edward reasoned, but he came forward all the same, stepping behind Charlotte so that she was being pushed against him. "If Alley Cat hadn't taken my phone –"

"Alley Cat?" Charlotte puffed raggedly, before biting her lip.

"You're distracting her," Jackson warned, so Edward obediently snaked a hand down Charlotte's top and into her bra, and another hand joined the action under her skirt.

"Maybe these corrupted people were put on this fine planet especially for us," Charlotte exclaimed between breaths. She arched backward against Edward, her eyelids fluttering. "Human aphrodisiacs."

Levering her higher, Jackson's love bites trailed over her collarbone, to the material of her bra and the nipple beneath it.

But after waves of Charlotte's enjoyment, and another heated taste of Edward too, even a jaunt with Mick the manservant … his friends were exhausted and more concerned about CARE, the murderess and the corrupted people.

On the other hand, the music was blaring in the club beyond the office and, unsated, Jackson had no choice but to allow himself to be pulled into one of the curtained rooms by Sherice and two of Charlotte's other girls, Darla and Chelsea.

Which was where he was, still cresting his high, with two of them kissing his bare chest, and the third kissing below the hip line – when the curtain was rippled by a newcomer, and the pulsing lights of the club behind her dazzled him for a moment.

Legs for days. Figure hugging leather pants. An off the shoulder crop. Dark hair pulled back. And sharp eyes zeroing in on his scantily clad company.

"Don't hurt them," Jackson managed, before Alley Cat reached forward and grabbed a handful of hair belonging to the girl crouched between his legs.

Her lips sucked free with a pop. He cried out at the loss of sensation. The girl cried out as she was torn backward, and the other girls whimpered as he suddenly shot up from the chair like lightning, pushing Alley Cat up against the velvety wall of the enclosed space.

"I said don't hurt them," Jackson repeated, pressing in against Alley Cat with an all new heated sensation as he saw the fire in her eyes. "Get out of here Chelsea, we're fine," Jackson told the nearest girl.

"Jax, I'm Kelsey," the girl sniffed tearfully.

"We don't care," Alley Cat spat in a low voice, her words like daggers.

With a nod from Jackson, Sherice, Darla and Kelsey skirted around the perimeter of the intimate room and hurried through the curtains. Before the curtains had settled Alley Cat had pushed him away from herself, and back into his chair.

He watched her, his chest heaving with desire as she stalked forward and straddled him like the first time. He reached around to squeeze skin tight leather, loving the feel of her.

"Deja vu," she simmered, and a thin knife that had appeared from nowhere was pressed lightly to his throat. "Ready for me to kill you again?"

"Will you be ready for me to come back?" he asked, his eyes dark and a playful smirk curling his lips.

"I'll kill you as often as it takes," she promised.

"I'll haunt you every time," he grinned wider.

"What are you?" she growled more intensely.

"Like you don't know," he teased in a low voice. "Aren't you employee of the month at CARE?"

She pulled back a little, frowning, and Jackson groaned as her seated weight jostled him.

"Aren't you the head of CARE, Mister White?" she challenged back.

"No darling," he answered, his eyes flickering to the zip that ran down the front of her crop. "I'm just a lonely shadow. Leader of none."

"Jackson –" the curtain rippled and Jackson cried out as Alley Cat moved against him again, this time angling another miraculously appearing knife toward Edward's gullet.

Edward's Adam's Apple bobbed as he swallowed. He had nearly stepped right into being murdered by her again.

"Some sobbing girls came to fetch me," Edward finished between gritted teeth.

"Don't worry," Jackson breathed. "She's got me right where I want me."

"You should be dead too," Alley Cat hissed, clearly disturbed.

"Oh, he was," Jackson promised. "For a little while. Why does CARE want us dead?"

Edward rolled his eyes. "I told you, Jax. I'm certain they are the good guys. She doesn't work for them."

"I don't work for them," Alley Cat agreed hotly. "But they are not the 'good guys' and I'm actively working to bring them down. Which is why you two were on the hit list. How did you manage it? Body doubles?"

"Now what a sight this is," Charlotte sighed as she slid past Edward then. "No wonder this one has my girls in hysterics again. She's gorgeous."

"She is," Jackson agreed, and then he risked leaning closer to Alley Cat, feeling the sting of her blade. "Do you think body doubles can explain my escape through your floor boards? Or those attackers with the dark eyes? It's clear I wasn't in league with them, and if you're against CARE, that must be where they came from."

She tensed. Her sense of logic warring with what she had seen and what had to be true.

"Very well," she answered silkily. "If this is legitimate, 'come back' again, and meet me at the National Museum before sun up."

Then in two swift motions she had sliced both Edward and Jackson's throats again.

Charlotte huffed and threw up her hands. "Woman, you are causing me no end of messes and cover ups."

Alley Cat rose from Jackson and glided to the curtains.

"You're familiar somehow too. But you aren't on my hit list yet," Alley Cat told Charlotte, eyeing her through a narrowed gaze. "I'm glad."

Then she was gone, disappearing through the heated, intoxicated crowd.

| 10 |

Mystery

Edward was rubbing his throat bitterly, but Jackson bounced up the steps to the vast National Museum with enthusiasm.

Its pillars and archways were lit up so that it looked like a mix between the White House and Greek architecture from the glory days.

"Beautiful," Jackson whistled, eyes on where Alley Cat had just stepped out from behind a pillar.

"Dangerous," Edward scowled.

"You made it," she remarked with a raised eyebrow. "This is becoming alarming."

"Wild horses and a knife through the oesophagus couldn't keep me away," Jackson assured her.

Alley Cat didn't shift. "Where's the red head?"

"Oh," Jackson shrugged. "You gave her girls a fright so she's dealing with that. Is this your new lair?"

"My employer's lair." Her eyes were still hard as she regarded them.

"And you suddenly trust us as guests rather than targets?" Edward questioned darkly.

"Only a fool would trust so easily. But the science doesn't lie," she shrugged, and then stepped aside to let them pass. "Walk ahead of me, in through the main doors. Head for the middle hallway at the end of the great entrance."

"I definitely feel welcome," Edward muttered as her gaze now bored into their backs.

"What do you mean, the science doesn't lie?" Jackson enquired.

They stepped across the darkened threshold into a grand room of soaring ceilings, framed masterpieces, gigantic models and lofty balconies. A colossal dinosaur's bones loomed in the middle of the room, and early Da Vinci style machines of flight hung from the roof. Great arched windows of stained glass cast starlight rainbows over the polished floors and books filled bookshelves that stretched endlessly upwards.

"I didn't clean my knives after killing you tonight," she stated. "My employer and I ran some tests."

"Oh?" Jackson's voice cooled an octave.

"Apart from some totally inexplicable results, we confirmed that you are not Mister White, the leader of CARE," Alley Cat admitted. "Turn left."

"Jax had told you that already," Edward stated dryly, stepping into a new wing of the gallery that was bursting with giant canvasses of nineteenth century art. "So what was it that convinced you?"

"Well, I had quite the full day today," Alley Cat told him in her low, velvety voice. "For instance, I killed you, Edward Scott, an apparent twin of Mister Knight – known deputy of CARE's leader. I was surprised to find who I thought was Mister Marcus Knight in this area, when I was certain that the assassination of CARE's supposed leader," she poked Jackson between the shoulder blades. "Would have caused chaos amongst the ranks, rather than inspiring casual travel. Left again here, and up the staircase."

"Hmf," Edward crossed his arms. But he did as he was told, and they climbed a staircase that circled a hall lined with statues and sculptures of all sizes and styles.

"Then I hacked the phone I stole from you, Edward Scott, and found recent alerts from your buddies in CARE. Those alerts suggested that no great panic had been raised at my recent murders – as if I had not taken out two of CARE's most important players. Go straight toward the staff only sign."

They had reached a well-stocked, luxurious library, but she simply led them on through a door marked for staff and they continued along a dimly lit corridor, sloping upward.

"Nevertheless, someone must have been watching you, Edward, because one of those 'good guys' with the unnatural eyes managed to surprise me while I still stood over your body with your hacked phone in hand. She got in one good swipe before I killed her."

"A poisonous swipe," Jackson surmised.

Her attention fixed on Jackson now. "When I woke to find you in my apartment, of all people – the first one I'd put down, and the leader of CARE, I felt certain you had come to slay me personally."

"Instead Jax took down your foes and nearly overdosed in the process," Edward stated.

"We'll get back to them. But when I killed you both again

tonight, I returned here, to where we have the very few items we have managed to pick up from Mister White. Using a strand of his hair and Jackson's blood on my knife we were able to discern that you are two different kinds of beings."

"Hallelujah," Edward glowered.

"Up the ramp," she answered, unbothered.

Simmering, Edward led the way. "I bet there is a more direct route to where we're going."

"Of course there is," she smirked. "I prefer you to be confused."

"You said Mister White and I are two different beings," Jackson mused. "That is odd phrasing."

"Would you prefer the term 'creatures'?" she asked. "Edward and yourself hardly appear to count as human, and Mister White even less so."

Edward gaped out from a door he had just pushed through. Jackson joined him on a landing, gazing down from where they stood at an internal balcony overlooking the level below. The walls of their level were filled with polished wooden shelves that brimmed with fascinating historical objects, but the level below was a massive space, dripping in screens and technology.

An illuminated world globe hung from the ceiling of their level and emitted enough warm, golden light for both levels – though the systems whirring below cast their own light too.

"Quite the advanced lair," Jackson commented.

Alley Cat took the lead then, and they followed her down a grand staircase to where a distinguished, bookish looking man with glasses and greying hair sat studiously reading a paper and sipping coffee among the screens. He was in a wheelchair, yet his broad shoulders and strong posture suggested he was a man of action.

Alley Cat crossed to the man and leaned against a bench beside him, crossing her arms, while he at last set the newspaper and coffee aside to regard Jackson and Edward thoughtfully.

"Welcome to the National Museum," he told them. "I am The Curator."

"We're going to want to know more than that," Jackson said, smiling languidly.

"You already do," The Curator answered. "This is a place that protects and shares treasures of the past so that humanity may understand and learn from its most glorious and inglorious events. That is our true goal. The goal of any institution such as this."

"Murder and espionage of course coincide with that goal quite naturally," Edward crossed his own arms and glared at Alley Cat.

The Curator wheeled himself across to a screen the size of a large home cinema. "They do, when unnatural organisations infiltrate every element of society, and threaten to eradicate knowledge of the past to control the future."

"Our kind do no such thing," Edward hissed. "We seek no such power."

Alley Cat sneered a little. "This is not about you – as it turns out. You are something else."

The Curator tapped some keys and a folder opened on the large screen. He selected one clip among many and the screen was filled with crystal clear footage of Jackson in a crisp, white suit heading a board meeting.

"Jackson Flint?" Edward breathed. "That's in CARE."

Jackson was frowning. "It does look remarkably like me. Except for the attire. Who wears a white suit? Completely impractical."

"Mister White is, at a glance, your twin," The Curator agreed.

"Which is why I was so confident in killing you," Alley Cat shrugged. "Though after studying both yourself and Edward, and your counterparts very closely, there are some subtle and interesting differences."

Jackson was watching his doppelganger's mannerisms keenly. "And what are those differences?"

The Curator paused the footage. "No face is completely symmetrical. Where yours differs in one way, his differs in the opposite. A slightly smaller left eye on you is a slightly smaller right eye on him. A freckle on your right hand is a freckle on his left."

"He's your opposite," Edward gaped.

"And it's the same with you and Mister Knight," Alley Cat informed Edward. She dragged the time of the clip forward to when a second suited man was standing to address the board room.

"Edward Scott," Jackson raised an eyebrow, intrigued. "I take it you never met these two power players or came face to face with our mirror images?"

Edward clenched his jaw, shaking his head. "I never met anybody who was not human."

"It's not like they took your tissue and cloned us," Jackson grimaced. "You don't rise to power so quickly. But where did these two come from? And why are they interested in pulling you into their organisation?" he asked Edward.

"As you say, these men are not recent to their leadership, and they are not your clones. From what we can discern, Mister White and Mister Knight have been at the head of CARE since it began," Alley Cat explained. "After the fall of Rome."

"The Dark Ages?" Jackson scoffed. "How in the world have we not come across these things?"

"And how in the world do you know all of this?" Edward questioned pointedly.

Alley Cat tilted her chin up, strong and cool as she regarded him. "I used to work for CARE. I was security for a while. Worked my way up to be body-guarding at the top. Mister White himself. Then I was chosen to head the treasure hunter team. I relished the adventure, the exotic places, the collection I was securing for CARE purposes. But I never seemed to find precisely what they wanted, and the items I did procure never resurfaced again. That got me thinking. That inspired me to really pay attention to who I was working for."

"And what did you discover?" Jackson asked. He was now lowering himself languidly into a nearby armchair.

"I discovered that CARE has access to, and ownership of information, organisations and places that no one institution should have. I discovered that, behind the scenes, they are infiltrating and shaping every element of the world. And I discovered that the highest leaders of CARE, in their position of growing power over humanity, did not appear to be human themselves. So I faked my death, and came to work for The

Curator to at least protect more artefacts from disappearing. And maybe chip away at CARE's power and supporters too."

Edward blinked at her. "You faked your death. You became a guardian of relics. You spied on CARE. And then murdered Jackson and I, thinking you had foiled CARE entirely?"

"You got it," Alley Cat answered flatly.

"No," Jackson shook his head. "You are more than a spying murderer. I've seen your work. And yet I feel no pure darkness or pleasure in death from you."

"She does feel ambiguous. They both do," Edward admitted begrudgingly.

"I'm a hobby assassin in my spare time," Alley Cat smouldered. "Usually I'm very good at it. Usually they stay dead."

"You put down some of my favourite snacks from around the world," Jackson smiled. "Not the kind of people that can be put down easily."

Alley Cat smiled back. "A hobby has to be interesting."

"Alley Cat was only selected to serve in CARE's security team, and then as their head treasure hunter, because she is gifted," The Curator elaborated. "She is a natural, whether in the field, or hidden on its fringes. It is not simple to disappear off such an organisation's radar."

"Until today," she muttered darkly.

"Alley Cat has been more than capable of hunting down CARE's top human associates – or your snacks, as you say," The Curator went on. "And she has even managed to steal some of CARE's security footage."

"So what do you add to the team?" Jackson eyed the man before him with interest.

The Curator rubbed a strong, closely shaven jaw. "I'm just the money. And the storage."

"And the man with the plan," Alley Cat added for him.

"Tell us, then," Jackson said, leaning forward with his elbows poised on his knees. "What is the plan in bringing us here?"

The Curator sighed. "We don't understand enough about who CARE are, where they came from, or what their intentions are. We reasoned that you might have a vested interest in investigating them too."

"And you feel that you do understand us, and trust us enough to work with you?" Jackson asked, a glint in his eye.

"In no way do we understand or trust you," Alley Cat reassured him silkily. "You came into this quite by accident. But you do not seem to be part of anything so large scale and so problematic as what CARE are, and if you're not with them – you might be convinced to be against them."

"I am yet to see any evidence that your little museum duo is any different to CARE," Edward said in a low voice then. "Both of you took my tissue and asked for better understanding. However, CARE never murdered me to take my tissue without asking."

"Aside from the fact that they hid your evil twin, Marcus Knight, from you," Alley Cat simmered, "There's this." She leaned over The Curator and opened a new clip. "Dated from this very day."

"Charlotte?" Jackson hissed.

"No," Alley Cat stated. "I've realised that your fiery friend has a mirror twin too. Marilyn Peace, director of affairs in the Southern Hemisphere."

"What's she doing?" Edward frowned. "Who is that with her, and what are they looking at?"

Two suited women stood peering down at a bench. One, Charlotte's copy, was facing the camera. The other woman had her back to it. But her outline was familiar enough after lifetimes of Edward and Jackson having known her. Her dark hair and skin, her narrow shoulders, her elegant poise.

"That's Jocelyn …" Edward swallowed.

"Or Anika Sweet – director of the Northern Hemisphere," Alley Cat supplied. "Which means that must be the Jocelyn you mentioned. Anika is examining her duplicate."

"No," Edward breathed. He was at last registering the slight shape of the unconscious woman strapped to the bench between the two suited females. The bright light shining down on the reflective bench had almost obscured her to the camera, but it was undeniably her.

"Why would they have Jocelyn strapped to a bench?" Jackson asked icily.

"For the same reason that two such prominent, international CARE leaders are now standing in the same room and country," The Curator answered. "CARE had so patiently been building intelligence on Edward. When their patience and trickery was wasted upon Edward's disappearance, they turned to the next obvious choice. The next one of his kin who came along in search of him. But they're not wasting time on niceties now."

Edward sank down against a desk covered in thick volumes, and Alley Cat's demeanour softened toward him at last.

"They want to study her and your kind," Alley Cat said.

"That may keep her safe for a while. And I'm guessing her lack of consciousness is simply a security measure."

"This has been a great deal for you to absorb," The Curator announced then. "But we do hope that you see your course of action – to understand where this threat has come from and what it is about, in fact aligns with our own goals. This group have been masters of pulling the strings from out of sight for too long. Will you join us in taking them down?"

"We're not heroes," Jackson answered. "We're the stark opposite. But we will be getting Jocelyn away from them, and we will be putting a stop to their threat to us. If you can be in some way useful to us in that venture – good."

The Curator nodded. "We definitely need each other's help on this. Alley Cat and I are good at what we do, but we are only human."

"Which brings me to one burning question," Alley Cat cut in. "What are you, and what do you bring to the table?"

"You already know. I am Edward Scott, this is Jackson Flint." Edward's eyes flickered to Jackson, waiting for his lead. Then Edward gazed unhappily back at the screen. "She is Jocelyn Truth."

"And once, not so long ago, I was Alexis Steel. Names can be researched further," Alley Cat replied calmly. "But I'd appreciate if you would save me the time and the misinformation."

"If we know some of your history and skill sets, we can plan accordingly," The Curator went on.

Jackson leaned back in the armchair. "Despite my admonishments of you earlier," he addressed Edward. "I believe the game has changed. We must let these two in. If they become an issue, we will darken their memories."

"Darkening memory," Alley Cat mused. "That's a start. Very useful. What else?"

A grin flickered on Jackson's face – a wily gleam in his eyes. "At the dawn of time the ill feeling that radiated from mankind was so tangible it birthed us." He disappeared from the armchair, reappearing beside Edward. "Now we draw the darkness from people to fuel ourselves," he circled Edward and then disappeared from sight again. "We are the darkness – darklings. Made strong enough by the corruption around us that we do not die." Jackson materialised between Alley Cat – or Alexis, and The Curator. He leaned on the desk between them. "We are energised by despair and debauchery. We are strong in physical form, are near untraceable in our shifting shadow state, and we move in sophisticated circles with our most succulent meals. So," his grin widened. "I'd say we have much to offer in the skill department."

"Excellent," Alley Cat commented without batting an eye. "Plenty to work with. I'm obviously not heading back to my apartment to sleep on all this, so I'll be in your bed," she told The Curator. "Are you coming?"

The Curator nodded and watched as Alley Cat stalked across the vast room to a side door that opened into his private living quarters. She disappeared without another word.

"I do my best planning in bed," The Curator told them. "With your talents, I'm positive that you can find your way back to your own beds tonight. Meet here again at dusk tomorrow, and we'll be ready to help your friend and take on CARE."

| 11 |

Alliance

"I obviously trust your judgment, Jackson," Charlotte had said before they'd left. "But don't kill my twin if she's as good looking as I am. What a waste that would be." Her face had been pinched with worry as they'd said goodbye.

Now Edward was quiet as Jackson led him, following their museum shadow traces from the night before. They were both too thoughtful to blur quickly along the ascending labyrinth of twists and turns to find the hidden office rooms.

But as they approached the final door Jackson grabbed Edward's belt loop and pulled him closer, wrapping an arm around the other man's broad shoulders.

"We'll get to the bottom of this," Jackson promised. And he thought of his own mirror image at the head of a board room, the dark eyed thugs, outsiders knowing about darklings, the fact that people seemed to be becoming rather vacant under CARE's leadership. And the fact that this not so new, but very surprising world scale group had Jocelyn. "We'll get to the bottom of all of it."

"Still no red head?" Alley Cat asked with slight disappointment when she spotted the two men entering the room above.

"Welcome back," The Curator greeted them, as smooth and unruffled as ever. He wheeled himself across to a central table with a screen tabletop and gestured for them to join him.

The screen was divided in two, showing a set of blueprints on one side, and a map on the other.

"We're going to split into two teams, with one team staying here at the museum as a base. Team one's focus will be on breaking into CARE's main buildings here in the city without being detected. We will use Alley Cat's blue prints and footage to help us, with the intention of secretly gaining intelligence, finding a way to destabilise CARE, and liberating Miss Jocelyn Truth."

"I will be in that team," Edward stated flatly, and The Curator nodded.

"Then Jackson will join Alley Cat in team two for a jaunt to Africa, where her last treasure hunt with CARE was, and where they have been continuously focusing their energies in search of something that can only be important."

Alley Cat was shouldering a compact bag, already smartly dressed for an undoubtedly first class flight overseas.

"I'm not adequately packed for our first trip together," Jackson frowned.

"I've got you covered," Alley Cat reassured him. "No passport required, and anything else we need we can pick up over there." She strode past him and shot him a smile so that he followed wordlessly, not mentioning that he could shadow his way across continents without such things as a passport.

The flight would give him time to talk to her.

He also got to be impressed as Alley Cat simply exchanged a few quiet words with the right people at the airport before they were escorted to the first class lounge, and then to their first class seats. No feathers were ruffled, no questions were asked, and it felt like no time had passed before they were in the air.

Jackson had to admit, while he could travel quicker in shadow form, human air travel had greatly advanced in comfort.

"The Curator must have some great friends," Jackson commented as Alley Cat reclined comfortably beside him. "A nod and a wink and you're off on a journey."

"Actually," Alley Cat raised her eyebrows, "I believe my face still comes up on their systems as being with CARE. They probably don't know what that means, just that it adds up to me having clearance to do anything I need to do."

"You're not worried that alarm bells will go off that a recently discovered alive, previously thought deceased CARE employee is back in action?"

"The airport didn't log anything, they just looked at my old profile," Alley Cat explained, accepting a bottle of water from the hostess. "And they didn't see that the border colour of my online ID was inactive grey, rather than a healthy, lively green. That's the perk of being in CARE. Nobody knows anything about them, they just know a CARE label means all access, no questions asked."

"I see," Jackson smiled as he accepted a crystal glass of golden liquor. "And what else can you tell me?"

"You know the same as I do now," Alley Cat replied. "Hence, the interstate mission."

"I meant about yourself," Jackson said. "About Alexis Steel," he rolled the name with a voice like velvet.

"She's dead."

"Before she was dead?"

"She had a quiet, unremarkable childhood, was terribly bored at school, and got noticed by a big bad organisation. She upskilled while working for them."

"No dark back story?" Jackson asked with surprise.

Alley Cat rolled to her side to hold him with her gaze. "Every choice in my life has been a conscious one. I haven't been pushed to be as I am because of some horrible past."

"You didn't get into the wrong scene to avoid that boredom at school?"

"I aced everything in school, excelled at every extra-curricular course I could take, and wanted a greater challenge," Alley Cat explained. "I wasn't coerced or fooled into joining CARE. I impressed them, and they offered me my next step."

"And faking your death when you decided to leave CARE?" he asked. "What about your family?"

Alley Cat took Jackson's glass from his fingers and swilled it, deeply breathing in the spicy scent before she returned the glass to him. "That," she admitted, "was regrettable. But it was best for them and for me."

Jackson whistled through his teeth. "You're quite unbothered by things that would bother most people."

"Can't change it. So why worry?" Alley Cat shrugged.

"CARE gave me a great funeral. Some real closure there. And I left all of my CARE savings to my parents. They've moved somewhere tropical." She lifted Jackson's free hand from his chair rest then, and drew his hand close to her face.

Jackson found himself holding his breath while her fingers turned his hand from palm up to palm down as she inspected him.

"Flesh and blood," she commented. "But also not. What else is there to know about you, Jackson Flint?"

He closed his fingers over hers, and with his other hand he tilted his glass forward to gesture at a guest seated further ahead in a side aisle.

The man was frowning deeply at his phone, with the red splotches that characterised growing anger starting to patchwork his neck and cheeks. But as Alley Cat watched on, Jackson focused more intently on the man, and with a slight inward breath Jackson began to draw on the bubbling anger heating the man's blood and balling in the man's stomach.

Tiny, almost invisible black spores lifted from the man and streamed back to Jackson, aiming for Jackson's chest. Alley Cat blinked and shivered as the specks disappeared into Jackson, while the man ahead visibly relaxed. The tension left the man's shoulders, the furrow left his brow and he loosened his tie, putting his phone away.

"So you're a healer of some kind. Darkling doesn't seem like the right name," Alley Cat mused. "Very subtle by the way. I only noticed because I was trying very hard to catch a trace of what you were doing."

"We're perfectly suited to the darkling name," Jackson defended in surprise. "You shivered as you felt that man's toxicity pass into me."

"Look how peaceful he seems now," she pointed out. "You drew out his demons."

"Hardly," Jackson scoffed. "He was just stressed about work. He tasted like papers and taxes."

"You caught a taste of him?" Alley Cat released his hand to draw her hair up into a ponytail. "What do your targets usually taste like?"

"My victims ... my prey," Jackson adjusted a perfectly positioned cufflink, "can taste like sour iced lemon when they are the cold, heartless type. They can taste like burning peppers that make your eyes water when they are the hot headed types. They're quick fix kinds of meals, the kinds you can just walk past and draw from by skimming the surface."

"And the others?"

"The murderers and real psychos leave a burn in your core, like the most acidic reflux. Taking a hit from them can leave them hollow, or dead, and leave you with a full, burning battery." Jackson set his glass aside and laid his head back against his chair. "Yet corruption – high end, straight up greed and self-service, tastes like rich, creamy chocolate. The kind you wish you could stop eating, and that makes you sick to your stomach. But that is too decadent to give up."

"Do you always just draw from people from a distance?" Alley Cat asked curiously.

"Contact helps – and hinders," Jackson grimaced. "Having a hold on your victim gets you deep access to every bit of what they have to offer. But a simple touch when you're not thinking can give you an unintentional taste of someone when you least desire it."

Alley Cat was laying on her side, her head cushioned by her hands as she listened. "Give me an example."

"A handshake can hit you with overwhelming energy if you're not being careful," Jackson explained. "And a kiss could turn an intimate moment into an invasion of that person that you never meant to make. We have to be separate and aware at all times."

"What could go wrong with a kiss?" Alley Cat smiled. "Unless you're terrible at it."

"Imagine getting swept up with someone, and then tasting a recent lie on their lips," Jackson said. "You're suddenly full, and the moment is broken as you wonder what they've been lying about."

"Yes, Edward mentioned that uncontrolled consumption nearly ended badly for you with those CARE goons," Alley Cat acquiesced. "But could a lie really taste as bad as corruption?"

"Some lies taste oily and greasy. They are so immoral they leave a slick feeling on your taste buds. Others, like little white lies or lies for the sweetest of intentions, are like sugar and strawberries. Either way, you taste a lie."

"I still think you're doing something good, by taking the worst out of people."

"Darklings have stood behind, and moved in circles with the worst people in history," Jackson disagreed. "We feed off the worst humanity has to offer and we flourish from it."

"Jackson," she said flatly, "you may shadow them. But you

don't become them. You're on a mission to bring down a potential threat to others right now."

"To save my own kind and to spend time with you," he
raised an eyebrow.

"Suit yourself," she smirked. "As you said, I'm neutral
enough that perhaps I have a clearer insight into this than you
do."

She rolled and stretched her back, closing her eyes.

He frowned and stared at the no smoking sign overhead.

| 12 |

Journey

"I can't believe you turned down that breakfast," Alley Cat shook her head as they passed through the cool of the bustling airport and out into the hazy heat.

She had shaken him awake upon descent, and while his shirt and face were unattractively lined with sleep wrinkles, she was as neat and pristine as ever.

"Don't worry," he muttered. "I skimmed myself a full meal on the way out here."

She was already headed to the pick-up bay, wearing sunglasses he could see himself in, and was scanning the crowds and cars.

"Not as filling a meal as the last time I was here though," Jackson ruminated, smoothing his hair.

"Oh?" she asked.

"Apartheid," he explained. "It gave me a stomach ache."

"Well, we're here on a search for something much less recent, historically speaking." She spotted a dusty, open-style jeep approaching in the distance and her face brightened.

Jackson's nose crinkled as the vehicle drew closer. "Of course. We're in Johannesburg. You don't come to the Cradle of Humankind for anything less than ancient history."

"We're not quite in the cradle yet," she answered, raising an arm to signal the beaten up car.

Jackson squinted to make out the car's equally dust covered driver, who was grinning from ear to ear. "I'm not sure we'll ever make it if you want us to go in that," he muttered. "Let me just turn you shadow with me for a bit and I'll get us across Gauteng province in a flash."

"Yes," she answered, but reached out to open the front passenger door as the car chugged loudly to a stop on the curb. "I plan to try that with you some time."

"Hey A.C!" the driver cried out with explosive enthusiasm. "I've missed you!"

Alley Cat swung herself into the seat and Jackson demurely took his place in the back.

"It's been a while Tiger," she replied warmly. "This is Jax."

"Hey man," Tiger twisted back to offer a dirty handshake. "Welcome to the place of gold!"

"I've been," Jackson answered dryly. "I started out near here. A long time ago."

Alley Cat gave Jackson a half smile over her shoulder while Tiger pulled out in front of the oncoming rush of airport traffic.

"It's of course more urbanised," Jackson sucked a luxurious breath in, tasting the air. "The population has grown. The city is beautiful. Hate crime is still a thing. But I don't take it we'll be staying here?"

"Too right, buddy!" Tiger cut in. "I'll have you out to the Sterkfontein Caves before the hour's up."

"You brought the things I asked for?" Alley Cat questioned, putting a hand on Tiger's bare arm.

Jackson noticed that Tiger's singlet clung to a rather toned body, and those exposed arms were tanned from a life of outdoor adventures. He was wiry – fit.

Jackson shifted uncomfortably in his buttoned shirt, adjusting the collar. The sun was beating down rather insistently.

"Yes ma'am," Tiger chirped. "You can't usually fly with hard-core CARE equipment like that!"

"CARE?" Jackson enquired with narrowing eyes. "How exactly do you know each other?"

"Tiger is quite the archaeologist and thrill seeker," Alley Cat explained. "He was working independently in the cave system when I came here with CARE."

"Those CARE chumps were swarming the caves, worming their way in without 'care' for what damage they were doing, and squeezing the university researchers and independents like me out," Tiger grimaced, zooming them down the highway. "They squeezed me right out of the main cave system and down into an untouched channel. They had no idea how close they were to something new."

"They had some idea," Alley Cat disagreed. "That's why they sent me to oversee the chumps."

"I'm not seeing how the two of you became friends," Jackson remarked, grabbing hold of his seat while Tiger roared off an exit and onto a straight road to more sprawling suburbs and then open lands.

"I was already feeling that my time with CARE, and as Alexis Steel, was coming to an end," Alley Cat sighed, holding her fingers out to catch the wind. "As it was, this became one of my last searches. I met Tiger one night. He didn't realise I was with them."

"I was too excited to have caught your attention," Tiger beamed.

"He showed me what trails he had found, and while we didn't know what was down there, we didn't want them to know either. At least not before we could work out the whole place's significance first," Alley Cat went on. "We knew it must be big. The kind of thing Mister White had been sending me out for since the beginning – because the tension for my team, and the pushing from above was crazy."

Gorgeous stretches of grasslands were blurring by now.

"A.C sabotaged the trail, deciding that the chumps should not discover or know what they so desperately wanted to know," Tiger said. "And I helped her to kill off Alexis Steel."

"How did you do that?" Jackson enquired.

"It took a small cave-in," Tiger grinned. "A cave-in that supposedly crushed A.C to death, while conveniently blocking all view of my little tunnel. Along with the new cave system I'd discovered beyond it."

"Then once I was safely dead and my team had moved on," Alley Cat took over, "we spent months combing through the new tunnel system."

"And?" Jackson leaned forward.

"And we found nothing," Tiger shrugged. "But it was still one of the best times of my life! Hanging out day and night with A.C, swapping stories and sharing –"

"You found nothing," Jackson repeated.

"We didn't have a friend with your skill set back then," Alley Cat placated Jackson, peering back at him with a meaningful expression.

"What exactly is your skill set?" Tiger questioned with interest. "Your suit makes you look like you'd be the money behind a project rather than an active player."

"Jax is great at getting in and out of impossible places," Alley Cat assured him, before shifting the topic. "But to finish the story of our grand meeting," she went on. "Tiger was the one who put me in contact with The Curator, so that when it was safe for me to resurface under the radar, I could keep working with someone as keen on learning about and protecting artefacts as I am."

"Man, it was a sad day letting you go to that next chapter of your life," Tiger sighed. "But the big cities aren't my thing, and the big cities are where you had to be to keep tabs on CARE."

"You would have hated the spy work," Alley Cat reassured him.

"The hit-woman work too?" Jackson asked slyly.

"Those aren't my kind of adventures," Tiger agreed amiably. "And besides, I had to spend some quality time in Tanzania. They must really think there's a chance that the Garden of Eden was there by the way," he went on. "With the first people out of Africa theory. Because CARE was right on my heels again, hoping that whatever they're searching for might be there instead."

"I hope they had no luck," Alley Cat glowered.

"Don't you worry," Tiger grinned. "They still seem to have

no idea what they're actually after. I even caught them watching and following me for leads. So I got out of there and took a break in Zimbabwe to shake them. I only left my Zimbabwe wanderings to make the trip to meet you with your things."

"You must have got in the car before The Curator had even hung up," Alley Cat grinned.

"Anything for you, A.C," Tiger agreed, following tourist bus signs that suggested they were nearing the caves.

"Well," Alley Cat said with a grin. "That's fortunate. Because I know the Witwatersrand science team would love to re-instate your passes and have you back to help. So we need you to get in and get our equipment in."

"Nice," Tiger beamed. "I can do that. They said I'd always be welcome."

"Meanwhile, I need you to turn off at that sign up ahead there," she told him, gesturing at a turn off signalling the Maropeng Boutique Hotel.

"Jax and I can't get in as legitimately as you can, so we'll be playing honeymooning tourists," Alley Cat added. "Mr and Mrs Flint can get lost on tomorrow's morning tour and meet you down in our secret caves where we used to camp."

Tiger's shoulders drooped slightly for just a moment. But Jackson noticed that the overall good feeling emanating from the young man didn't waver with the taint of jealousy that one could expect.

Instead, Tiger appeared to be simply and genuinely pleased with what time he could get with Alley Cat, and with whatever thrills that would entail.

Begrudgingly, Jackson decided he liked the young explorer.

And Jackson liked him even more when he had dropped them off outside the luxury hotel, disappearing in a haze of dust while Jackson himself was led to a nice honeymoon suite with Mrs Flint.

| 13 |

Desire

They had made themselves blend in, the happy couple touring the nearby visitor centre.

Alley Cat had held his hand and arm, leaning into him lovingly so that cool waves had rippled across every point of contact between them and right into his core.

He had struggled to take in 'the boat ride of creation and evolution', and had only drawn a full breath in after they had crossed the gleaming hotel lobby to return to their room, and she had released his hand to go to her bag.

"It was not so bad being Mrs Flint today," she remarked lightly.

"I should think not," he managed, leaning in the open back doorway.

Their apartment opened out to a view of the sweeping ranges. It was as if a guest could step out among the South African grasses and keep walking across rocky planes, over mountainous rises and under open skies until they had traversed the whole continent.

"Any wife of mine would have no complaint," Jackson added, turning from the view in time to see Alley Cat shimmying into a black satin dress. It slid over a taut stomach and draped in a cowl over her chest. It ran down her body like water, its short hem sweeping her mid-thigh.

"Should I have told you that I'd kill you if you peaked?" she smirked, turning to the gleaming bathroom and twisting her hair up so that the drop in the back of her dress could be fully appreciated.

"Only if you could wait for reanimation," Jackson replied, cocking an eyebrow as he noticed a crisp black suit hanging on the back of the wardrobe door in wait of him. "But you haven't eaten since breakfast, and since you can't skim from the people around you, I can guess you're too hungry to wait that long for dinner."

"Famished," she agreed. "So hurry up and change. We'll dine immediately."

He approached the suit and raked it appreciatively with his eyes as he took it down.

"Beautiful," he murmured, stepping into the new trousers with relish.

"I think you'll find I did a good job of sizing you up Mister Flint," Alley Cat announced, coming to stand behind him as he fastened the belt. She stood so close that the warmth seemed to radiate from her and to shiver up his spine.

"Impeccable job," he breathed as she took the shirt from its hanger and began to help him into it.

Jackson felt her fingers brush against the backs of his arms as they passed into the sleeves, then he felt her fingers run over his chest as she circled around him. With a wicked gleam in her dark eyes she buttoned his shirt, working her way down to his naval while he felt the traces of her passing touch on his skin.

He tucked the shirt in while she flicked up his collar and turned to collect the black tie that had been set out. Then she looped it around his neck and tightened it just enough, making a smart loop and smoothing the tie and collar in place.

"Sharp," she purred. "You'll pass for a husband."

When they were seated to dine he gripped his chilled glass, grateful for the ice in the scotch.

She questioned him throughout the meal, but half of his attention was on every expression and move she made.

"What are your memories of your start?" she asked at last, toying with the rim of her own chilled glass of water. "Was our tour today like a walk down memory lane?" She crossed one long leg over another. "Were people – and were you – really like that?"

Jackson stared at the flame of the candle dancing between them for a moment. A frown furrowed his brow.

"I suppose they were. And I suppose we were," he answered. "Darklings were born from the first negative deeds and feelings of humanity, but we were born as raw and ignorant as any being is born. We looked like ourselves, but also not. We had to evolve too."

"Even you," she eyed him with interest, "you began in a primitive state? Like those first human models we saw today?"

He shrugged. "The first humans were most of the time such mindless creatures that they didn't have either good or evil intent – just instinct for survival and functionality. I was indistinct, a jumbled presence only gaining tangible strength as the corruption and selfish motives of people developed."

She thoughtfully took a sip of her water.

"Your hazy beginnings may explain why you were not aware of others. Such as Mister White and CARE," she mused. "And they may also explain why CARE itself is so determinedly seeking answers of its own."

"Perhaps that's why CARE are only going after their darkling counterparts now," Jackson agreed. "They may have only just become aware of us too, with the help of this modern, technological age."

"C A R E," Alley Cat drawled the word bitterly. "Whatever their reasons, whatever they're really doing by taking so much control … I think they've become worse than the dark force that birthed you at the beginning."

"What does CARE even stand for?" Jackson asked curiously. "Corrupting And Ruining Everything?"

A smile flickered at the corner of Alley Cat's lips. "Corporation Alliance for Resources and Energy," she answered. "Basically – a business that binds all businesses together and owns everything."

"They definitely took a different approach to life than the darklings did," Jackson remarked. "At different times we've banded together in small groups. We understand and love each other. But we are independent creatures – consuming and devouring for the fun and for our need of it."

Alley Cat uncrossed her legs and set her glass aside. The windows behind her were dark, but for the glittering of the stars.

"I'm done caring about CARE for tonight," she smouldered. "I think we should consummate the marriage."

Jackson contemplated her seriously. "I think we should take things slowly."

This time the smile plucked at her lips more strongly. "Let's see who wins."

| 14 |

Burning Up

She had drawn him up from the table. She had drawn him all the way back to the room, which was lit only by the silvery light of the night, pouring in from the still open glass doors.

Alley Cat's speed in closing the front door and then pushing him up against it would have shocked others. But he smiled against her intense kisses as they forced him backward. He felt her bite playfully at his bottom lip, and then she pulled at his shirt so that it untucked from his trousers – ready to rip it open.

"Wait," Jackson said in a low voice, growling huskily.

In a moment she had rotated him away from the door, spring boarding him to the bed.

He sat up, propped up on his elbows.

"Slow down," he told her with upward quirking lips.

Panther-like, Alley Cat stalked toward him. "I told you, every choice in my life has been a conscious one. Why hesitate?"

She sat herself on his lap, thighs either side of him, lips at his neck.

"Because I am not just some boy to be used. I am not to be trifled with."

He put his hands on her thighs. Holding them with a little pressure.

"Of course not. You are to be enjoyed. Devoured."

He moved one hand down one thigh and then down the length of her leg, still holding that pressure.

"I have been enjoyed and devoured throughout the ages," Jackson whispered. "Sweaty tumbles can be fun. But with you," he reached the end of her leg. He slowly drew one stiletto off. "With you, I want to explore and experience everything I can."

Then his second hand moved down her other leg. Squeezing lightly. Inch by inch.

"Every touch and every movement counts." He slid her second stiletto off.

"I see," Alley Cat murmured. "We're taking this seriously."

"Deadly."

Jackson stood, so she had to stand too. Close. He guided her hands to rest on his narrow hips, and his eyes locked on hers.

He let his own hands brush softly down her shoulder blades and bare back, down the slippery material of her dress to the hem.

He very carefully, very slowly lifted the hem of the dress – its satiny material trickling its way up her athletic body. The slippery touch of the cool fabric and his passing knuckles left a trail of spreading goosebumps that rose on her skin and hardened her nipples as she allowed him to pull the dress over her head.

Jackson put a hand to the back of her neck, squeezing at the nape of her hairline and angling her face to his.

His lips were warm against hers.

Still gripping her hair, he tilted her head so he could kiss from her jawline to her neck, to her collar bones and down, over a pert nipple.

"I admire how brazen you are. Taking control," Alley Cat breathed against him. "But I always go after what I want. And I always get it."

She reached up and, button by button, undid his shirt.

Her eyes took in Jackson's firm stomach and defined chest before she forced the shirt back from his shoulders and free of his arms.

She raked her fingernails down his torso and took hold of his belt, easing it undone. Then she leaned in, pressing against him as she slowly dragged his zip all the way down.

"It's good for you not to get what you want straight away," he told her.

Alley Cat ignored him, drawing his trousers and her body downward until she kneeled in front of him.

"I can quite clearly tell that you want it too," she purred.

But he stooped and swept her up.

Surprising her, he turned them both momentarily shadow, blurring them across so he could lay her on the bed.

"You left your trousers, shoes and socks over there," she managed as he levered himself over her.

"I let them stay physical, so they didn't come with us," he began. "But let's not get into the mechanics of it."

"Let's not," she agreed, and reached for the bulging area of the one item of clothing he still wore.

"Mine are staying on," he told her. "Yours won't be."

Jackson leaned in to press his lips against hers, feeling her bare chest against his. Her legs brushed against his and her arms wrapped around his bare shoulders.

But then he pulled back, taking her arms away from him and holding her wrists up on the pillow with one hand.

With his other, he traced his fingertips over her hips, her naval, her ribs, her neck and up to her trapped wrists in a continuous line.

He released her wrists and moved so that he could touch his mouth to her skin with light kisses, and sometimes light bites.

She arched up against him with a moan as Jackson's teeth pinched and his tongue played on the buds of her nipples, each flick of movement sending bolts of pleasure through her.

He traced the waistline of her underwear with his fingers moving under the elastic suggestively and she tilted her hips so that he could drag them down.

She gasped when his touch roved back upward and his fingers slid between her legs – his hand clasping her sex entirely and moving up, down and diagonally on her most sensitive point, or rubbing in circles while he continued his attention on her breasts.

When he felt her hands settle absently in his hair, he slid his fingers inside her to add to the sensation, drawing both his fingers and palm against her sensitive places now, and upping the regular pace to match her audible breaths.

He toyed with her with growing satisfaction until she was undeniably building to her climax, rocked far beyond control and totally at his mercy for her pleasure.

He pushed away from her heaving breasts and put all of his attention toward her swelling waves of passion, his hand pressing, rubbing and not relenting or changing in rhythm until she at last gave up a cry of complete abandon, throwing her head back against the pillows and grasping his biceps, her hips driving up against his hand and her body rigid.

He angled himself upward to press a more fiery kiss against her lips as her body settled back to relax warmly against him. He pulled her closer and drew a silken sheet over them so that it felt like cool liquid against their heated skin.

She grinned up at him and then rested her cheek on his smooth chest. "Alright. You won that round."

| 15 |

Business

"Good morning," Jackson said, still languishing on the bed as Alley Cat sauntered in from the bathroom, wearing his mostly buttoned up shirt and some boy-leg underwear.

She sat herself in an armchair across from the bed, one leg drawn up on the seat.

"Last night was the least physical I've ever been with a man," she stated. "But it was the most intimate."

Jackson eyed the new trousers and shirt she'd hung on the wardrobe door for him. Less formal, and grey in colour. Durable, but still smart.

"What about with The Curator?" he asked curiously, without jealousy. "I assume his paraplegia means he relies on similar methods to what I used?"

"He is quite able to get an erection, and our jaunts together are pretty saucy," she admitted. "But with him the focus has always been on experimentation. I treat him like I'm his sex rehab nurse while we discover what works."

"Fun," Jackson commented. Now slightly jealous. "Perhaps the difference is that my sole focus was on you."

She nodded. "It drove me crazy at the start," she mused. "But you really wanted to be with me in the moment. To focus on and feel me."

"You can't rush art," he replied. "We can learn about each other as we go."

"Thank you." She stood, thoughtful for a moment. "For now, though, I need you dressed, washed and ready to be the happy touring couple again."

"Right. Back to business."

She eyed him candidly as he rose and the sheet fell away. Then her lips quirked and she turned back to her bags, pulling the shirt over her head and selecting a black tank top and fitted, flexible pants to wear.

When he was ready, she held out her hand to him and he accompanied Mrs Flint to the lobby to await the bus. He was still holding her hand even as they were herded off the bus among a group of tourists, and were led down the stone steps and into the dark entrance of the caves.

"We are very careful with our security at this heritage site," the guide was saying to the tourists at the front. "You must not approach any gates or leave the tour trails at any time."

"I'm assuming that's exactly what we're going to do," Jackson murmured as they were led along a tight walkway and out into a well-lit cavern with a soaring ceiling.

"Of course," Alley Cat replied quietly, making sure they were at the back of the group. "Tiger's tunnel entrance is on the other side of the underground lake. We'll slip away when the group heads towards the boardwalk and gets distracted by the original excavation site."

"You know," the tour guide said, pausing to point at green moss growing on a rock wall. "Scientists believe this moss may have been where the first forms of life evolved from!"

There were exclamations and camera flashes as the crowd pushed forward.

"You know, to dispel the greasy flavour from a comfortable gangster last month, I dangled him off the Statue of Liberty." Jackson spoke easily and casually, like all the other happy sightseers. "The taste of terror was exhilarating, and I had absolutely no heartburn after I'd drained him."

"You know, I once scaled a skyscraper with only a pair of untested grip gloves and experimental grip shoes from CARE," Alley Cat countered.

"I can shadow my way over buildings … and continents," Jackson commented smugly.

"I enjoyed killing you both times," Alley Cat shrugged. "And Edward too. But Charlotte was too pretty to spoil."

"I see," Jackson laughed softly. "You win. Shall I darken the group's memories? They'll have no recollection of us being here."

"The moss wins as most impressive," she grinned. "But yes."

The water, when they reached it, was clear and blue in the lights cast in the cavern. But the end of the lake was in shadows and their view of the other side was obscured by stalactites dripping down toward the water surface.

"Did you ever darken my memory, Mister Flint?" Alley

Cat asked in a low voice, standing on the outer edges while the rest of the group listened carefully to the guide.

"I never did," he admitted. "Though if any other darkling had allowed a human to really know them, I would have hunted that darkling down and ended them permanently myself."

She raised an eyebrow. "You deal darkling justice?"

"I do what I do and others always seem to listen and follow," he shrugged. He pressed his hand to the small of her back and held her close so that they looked like they were whispering sweet nothings.

"But I couldn't darken your memory – I wanted you to find me again. So that I could learn why you were targeting us. And also just so that you would find me again."

She smirked. "How exactly does it work, to darken someone's memory?"

Jackson rolled his shoulders. "Watch." He narrowed his eyes and focused on the people closest to them. "I send out the faintest traces of shadow, and let them seep into the target's brain – right where the memory lives."

Alley Cat noticed an almost imperceptible shifting in the air, like waves of heat that dance above the surface of a road on a scorching day.

"I guide the shadow to go deeper, to pinpoint and then to make a blur over the images of our faces in that person's memory," he went on, speaking softly beside her ear as the rippling in the air washed over the next few rows of people. "And they forget the specifics about us. Soon we blend in among the dark patches of their minds." The rippling waves made it all the way to the guide. "Soon we are gone from their minds altogether."

Jackson stepped behind her then, and pressed her back against himself, wrapping his arms around her as if in an embrace.

Alley Cat's breath caught, and suddenly he turned the two of them to shadows themselves.

"Right!" the tour guide's chipper voice called. "Have we got everyone?" he craned to look, doing a head count and squinting directly at them. Through them. Counting as if they'd never been there.

"Ok, let's keep going! Next you'll see where the oldest fossils of our early ancestors have been found."

Alley Cat felt as if she were both real and not real. Physical, but untethered. Yet she felt shivers run through ... whatever she was in this state ... when Jackson lowered his barely tangible lips to press a kiss to the top of her barely tangible shoulder.

Before she could really think about any of this though, Jackson had lifted them up as if they were nothing but cloud, and they were skimming quickly over the water surface – its mirror not showing their passing reflection.

When they reached the darkened edges of the great pool Jackson made them tangible again so that they stood at the banks, and Alley Cat couldn't help but hold his arm tightly, her eyes wide.

"The entrance is underwater," she panted. "It isn't for long though. It curves up like an S bend and becomes a dry tunnel that opens into a new system of caverns."

"Ah," Jackson sighed. "The glory of being the first darkling to pass through a natural toilet."

"It's over there," she nodded to a section of cave wall that appeared to be exactly the same as everywhere else.

"Unfortunately, we're going to get wet," Jackson told her. "The water particles mess with my shadow particles and I don't want there to be any risk to you."

"I think I prefer being physical again for now," Alley Cat admitted, feeling grateful as they waded into the chill of the lake before separating to tread their way across the water.

"Big breath?" he asked.

"Big breath," she affirmed. "But it won't be for too long."

Alley Cat took his hand and guided him to the wall. With a nod from her, they both drew their breath in and dived, feeling with outreached fingers for the opening in the rock.

Jackson felt a squeeze of pressure from Alley Cat as she located their tunnel, and she started to pull him forward to follow her into the cold, silent passage of water. He felt the ancient rock encircling them, and the effort of their confined movements. But before his lungs were strained, Alley Cat was angling them back upwards and they were surfacing on a rocky, track-like slope.

"Tiger did that with all of your equipment?" Jackson asked, wiping water from his eyes.

"If all went to plan," she nodded, stepping out of the water and pulling him up. "Tiger is a very experienced explorer though. He would have tied it all to himself and found his way. Hopefully he now has a warm fire roaring so we can dry off."

She smoothed her slick hair back and led the way along the semi-dark passage, which grew lighter as they continued.

"See, he's left something burning ahead in the first main cave," she announced, heading for where the passage opened out into a spacious cavern again.

There was a well built, contained bon-fire sending out radiant heat and light, and packs of equipment stacked neatly to the side. But no Tiger.

"I was expecting an 'A.C' welcoming party," Jackson commented, eyeing the massive space and how the shadows of jutting rocks danced in the firelight. Many other, smaller tunnels opened up here and there, and one side of the cavern appeared to drop suddenly with a ledge over an abyss.

"He would have gone off exploring," Alley Cat explained, unconcerned as she rifled through one of the water-tight bags. She pulled out a couple of large water canteens and put them in a smaller backpack, along with a handful of muesli bars, a fancy looking fluoro pen, tube lights, and a couple of odd devices.

"I guess we won't be needing the usual ropes, harnesses and carabiners if I have you to help me," she speculated. Though she pulled on a pair of professional climbing shoes and packed her grip powder just in case.

Her skin suit pants had already nearly dried, and her damp hair was sitting in loose waves above her shoulders. Jackson, still soggy and with less of an adventurer's spirit, sat close to the fire while she roamed the cavern, inspecting different tunnel and cave openings.

"I've found where Tiger must have gone," she told him as she returned to the fire at last. "There are a few hard to reach openings in the rock on the other side of that ledge. He's left some lines anchored in that would have helped him to get across."

"Of all the accessible rock openings in this cavern," Jackson frowned. "Why did he choose the openings that are across an abyss?"

"The challenge," she grinned. "We only did one of those ones together in the past, so he's trying his luck in another now."

"Daredevils," Jackson muttered.

"I'm not as interested in the high up or abyss openings this time though," she mused. "Even though we did most of these lower tunnels and caves, we didn't have your skill set, as I've mentioned before."

"I don't fancy carrying you through rock walls," Jackson warned. "We could find ourselves trapped in the stone."

"Still," Alley Cat went on confidently, "if we're searching for something truly ancient, these lower openings may be the best place to start. Not too low – they would have formed from water erosion over time. But not too high – they would be more recent."

"So the middle is just right," Jackson affirmed.

"Last time there were a few passages that the scanners picked up on, but that had been blocked by fallen rocks or that were on the other side of closed off walls. They could be good to go over now."

"Part of the stone wall forever," Jackson reiterated darkly.

"Right," she nodded, shouldering her pack. "Let's get started, shall we?"

She scaled her way up to a gaping tunnel entrance that opened five meters off the ground.

He shadowed after her.

And for hours they branched out and circled around the winding passages, with only arrows from her special highlighter pen allowing them to see where they had been and which way was back. They hadn't come across any of the mysterious, blocked passages Alley Cat had hoped for.

"We should probably return to base," Alley Cat finally announced, pocketing her scanner in disappointment. "The glow of the highlighter fades after eight hours, and we don't want to lose our way."

"We've nearly been eight hours?"

"This was a smaller tunnel system," she affirmed. "And we covered ground quickly."

The fire had burned away when they dropped back into the main cave, and there was still no Tiger. Alley Cat remained unworried, certain that her friend must have chosen to camp on the track.

So they rekindled the fire and shared a meal of tinned, unidentifiable food before rolling out two sleeping bags.

"Do you get as many thrills working for The Curator as you did working for CARE?" Jackson asked.

She rolled to face him, resting a cheek in her hand as she considered it.

"I have power over what I'm doing, and I'm not weighed down by processes or lackeys anymore. Ambitious ladder climbing could only interest me for so long."

"Your morals interest you more now?"

Alley Cat thought about it again. "This way I get to keep

my morals, my freedom, and do as many crazy stunts as I used to. But I can operate in a grey area – utilising a lot of CARE tech and know-how that I hoarded over my time."

"The medical kit back at your apartment was pretty high grade," Jackson agreed. "And you had quite the stash of price-less artefacts."

"At the time I was stowing them away because I thought they might be what CARE were after. Then it was out of spite and personal desire," she shrugged. "But one day they could join The Curator's public or studied collection, if we sabotage CARE control and can be open again."

"So we really have no idea what we are searching for in the meantime," Jackson mused.

"I feel like we'll know it when we see it," Alley Cat sighed, laying back. "It has to be related to the earliest history, based on their searches. And it has to contain some kind of helpful knowledge to them."

"What could possibly help them, when they already have all the power any organisation could want?" Jackson mused.

"They have their power. But now their concern will be to do with keeping it. There must be something out there that they plan to use, or that can be used against them."

"Well," Jackson leaned across and pressed his lips firmly against hers, tucking her hair behind her ear. Then he settled back to sleep. "I'm sure we'll work it out, find what we're af-ter, learn why they're targeting darklings, and bring down their power system tomorrow."

| 16 |

Surprise

"Do you need to sit down?"

"No," Alley Cat grimaced stubbornly, straightening from where she had leaned against the rock wall nauseously. "We're getting better at this."

They had traversed two more cave systems, and after Alley Cat's insistence, had been experimenting with passing through solid rock to get to the other side of any blocked tunnels.

The first time had nearly seen them both stuck – unable to go forward through the dense stone. Fortunately Jackson had still had enough essence left spread out as an anchor on the surface of the rock, that he had been able to re-trace and suck them all the way back out.

The second time he had thought long and hard about an alternative. Then he had shrunk them down to the smallest wisp of smoke-like shadow, and had carefully issued them into and along a slight fissure in the rock. The process had been a long, slow one – easing their way along the tiny, delicate webbing of cracks in the hopes that they would eventually find a path that went all the way through to the other side.

The risk had paid off, but they had found nothing, and had had to repeat the process a few more times already. After the most recent transition, Alley Cat was struggling to feel like a physical being again.

"I'll be quicker getting us back out this time," Jackson reassured her. "I'm pretty sure I remember the crack lines that worked."

"Let's not think about going through that again just yet," she replied, her face pale and pinched. "New tunnel, new steps forward. Let's go."

He didn't argue, but took hold of her hand to make her feel anchored to the real world all the same, and she held onto him a little more tightly than she normally would have as she left her glowing arrows on the walls.

They had both quietly started to feel this tunnel was as useless as the others – with Jackson now dustier than he ever had been in his life, when Alley Cat paused ahead of him.

"What is it?" he asked. He was unable to see around her in the narrow passage they had now reached the end of.

She was frowning. "We're about to step out into a large cavern," she said. "But the rock colourings are different."

"We've probably crossed into a whole new part of Africa," Jackson drawled. "Perhaps they have different rock foundations."

He squeezed out after her and squinted at the oddly coloured patches of rock while she fished for a brighter light stick.

He only paid the rock colouring more heed when she lifted the light and drew in her breath sharply.

"They're paintings," Alley Cat said wonderingly. "Cave paintings from the earliest people. They must be."

"Unless of course we walked all the way to an African art gallery by mistake," Jackson mused. But he was transfixed by the clearly ancient display. "They're not the usual kind of stick figures you find from pre-history."

"It seems to start in the middle. Up there," Alley Cat gestured, lifting her light to the centre of the high ceiling.

"You're suggesting the ancients had a sense of story?" Jackson frowned, but he could see that she was right. There was a larger scene drawn in the middle of the uneven rock surface, and the others seemed to flow out from it.

"I've never seen anything like it," Alley Cat breathed. "And nobody else must have ever seen them either. Nobody else could have got down here. They have to be older than the other fossils and artefacts found in these caves – and everything found here is supposed to be the first of everything from the earliest people to have ever existed. But these are so detailed. Almost sophisticated."

"Thank you," a new voice cut in. "I'll pass your compliments on to the artist, Mister White."

Jackson and Alley Cat whirled back to the impossible place of their entrance, where nobody should ever have been able to follow them.

But standing there behind them was Edward. Or, not Edward. Mister Marcus Knight. Along with Tiger, whose eyes were entirely black.

"And you're right, these have been quite hard to find and

have remained undiscovered much too long," Marcus Knight went on, while Tiger stood oddly inert beside him. "Without you two leading the way we never would have worked out how to get here. Tracing cracks in smoke form was genius."

"I thought so." Jackson crossed his arms.

"Tiger?" Alley Cat tried to get some kind of recognition from her friend.

"Yes, Tiger did his best," Marcus sighed. "He is great at what he does. We've been tracking his work in finding the Garden of Eden, but what we were looking for wasn't there. It was here. And it turns out so are you, alive and well, Miss Alexis Steel. The greatest in your field."

"What did you do to him?" Alley Cat asked coldly.

Marcus smiled, turning to eye Tiger's stiff form. "I took ninety nine percent of his goodness. So he's a potent follower to have. I don't need a thinker now that I've got you Alexis."

"You haven't got her," Jackson reminded Marcus with a smile of his own.

"Miss Steel, I really am so glad that you're not dead," Marcus went on, circling around now as if to peer at the cave drawings. "But what have you become without CARE? You're just a call sign, working with hidden, divided players … working with darkness. You'll wind up on the wrong side of history if you work with such a villain."

"Forgive me," Jackson countered. "But in terms of villains, who out of the two of us reduces a person to complete evil?"

"I told you," Marcus glared at Jackson now. "Tiger has one percent of his goodness left. Or he'd be dead."

"Why not kill him then?" Alley Cat hissed. "Why take him

through the cracks with you when we know how hard that is?"

"A good minion is always useful, especially seeing as Mister Flint here got rid of a number of our twenty-percenters at your apartment Miss Steel," Marcus waved a dismissive hand.

Jackson straightened with a stony expression. "They were only eighty-percent dark?"

"Oh yes," Marcus replied pleasantly. "And coming in contact with them didn't really agree with you, did it?"

"Can what you have done to Tiger be reversed?" Alley Cat asked in a low voice.

"I like how I am now, A.C," a monotone voice came from Tiger then. "I'm not worried about anything anymore."

"See," Marcus shrugged. "It is the lightling gift. Everyone we touch becomes happier, and we mean to touch the world. You are on the wrong side, Miss Steel."

"Theoretically," Jackson grunted, "if 'lightlings' are like us they can both fill a person and drain a person. I would expect it could be reversed."

"Tiger," Marcus said conversationally. "Show them how happy you are. And why Alexis should work with me on this."

Tiger moved with inhuman speed, lunging straight for Jackson like a torpedo to the chest. They both crashed down, with Tiger pinning Jackson against the ground and immediately raining a torrent of upward punches into Jackson's ribs and face. Each blow sent shattering, overwhelming waves of darkness into Jackson so that the darkling groaned.

With a bland expression Tiger ripped at Jackson's shirt, exposing bare skin for full contact, and smashed his knuckles directly into the centre of Jackson's chest as if to directly flood Jackson's heart.

Aside from the physical trauma, the dangerously addictive, seductive overdose being forced into his body filled Jackson until he was ready to snap like an elastic band.

Baring his teeth with the effort, he seized Tiger's shoulders and threw his attacker off with such force that Tiger arced across the cavern and hit a wall.

"Jackson!" Alley Cat warned urgently, "you said he could be saved!"

Jackson, looking so wired that he might catch fire, still managed to pause to listen to her. And in that pause, Tiger blurred his way back into Jackson – hitting him with a bone shattering kind of tackle.

"He's barely human now," Jackson cried out.

"If you're not careful," Marcus Knight remarked. "You'll lose them both. Jackson will get stronger and stronger until he is overwhelmed by the thing that makes up his very essence. There's no coming back from that. And Tiger will keep doing as I bid until they both smash themselves apart."

Alley Cat shot the lightling a withering glare. "And what can I do to prevent that?"

"In the short term, authenticate, document and analyse what we're seeing in this cave. Quickly – for their sake," Marcus explained. "In the long term, come back to CARE without me having to use a brain numbing compulsion. You need to realise that you are working with incredibly volatile, dangerous creatures. The darklings must be controlled. You can help us to help the world."

"Short term sounds acceptable," Alley Cat glowered,

knowing that she needed to gain time and that she had very little choice but to agree. "Seeing as I was going to do that anyway."

She lowered her backpack to the ground and pulled out a scanner, all the while trying to ignore the meaty sounds of Jackson now trying to incapacitate Tiger in the background.

"That is an outdated model Alexis," Marcus sniffed. "If you'd still been working for CARE you would be properly equipped for such important work."

Ignoring the meaty sounds and Marcus Knight, Alley Cat began a panorama style scan of the cave, working from the centre and outward as the images seemed to flow. In spite of Marcus' words, Alley Cat's scanner was near state of the art in its capabilities – picking up each dimly lit, shadowy image clearly.

She placed the small scanner on an upward jutting rock for a table, letting it begin a sequencing program that would seek to find meaning in and to organise the images. For a moment Marcus watched the flashing images on the screen as they were sorted, but his sharp gaze shifted to Alley Cat when she next took a scalpel and a finger-sized test tube from a kit in her pack and crossed briskly to scrape a painted sample of the rock into the tube.

Conveniently, she had stopped by a rock wall that was relatively close to Jackson and Tiger. They were both quite battered, with Jackson now visibly reigning himself in as if he might explode, while on the other hand Tiger was tiring.

Jackson's eyes were glittering with energy, his whole body was taut with the ecstasy of it and dark veins stood out on any un-bloodied skin. He did look the image of uncontrollable, wicked glee as he lifted Tiger by the throat and threw his own head back with a laugh.

"I'm not even trying to absorb it – the dark is just radiating from this guy," Jackson yelled.

"Just hold on," Alley Cat told him levelly, though she could tell he was on the brink of being too far gone. "Wait for my signal. And don't kill my friend."

"Yes ma'am," Jackson cackled. His veins were rippling.

"The scanner has produced a file, Alexis," Marcus called. He moved to touch the device as she crossed back with her sample.

"Don't," she warned him sharply. "I've configured that device to accept only my touch or to self-destruct."

"Of course you have," he rolled his eyes.

"But you are welcome to watch me entering the address for where the data file will be sent to," Alley Cat added coldly. "For the sake of trust and you calling Tiger off."

She made sure to appear uncomfortable as he stepped behind her to watch over her shoulder. But instead of reaching for the scanner, she swiftly pivoted and planted her scalpel in his chest.

She pushed the little blade in as far as it would reach without making the very end of the handle slippery, and it sliced through his tissue as if it were air. Then she rapidly plucked it free and criss-crossed his chest again, to really give his heart some nice carvings. For good measure, she nicked both of his wrists, and he was still only now slumping to the floor with a shocked, glassy-eyed expression.

"That's not your signature move," Jackson crowed, throwing a now unconscious Tiger over his shoulder. "But I take it that's the sign!"

"I'd like to see him bounce back from that death in a hurry," Alley Cat replied, slipping her scanner and test tube into a protective case and pocketing them. "You ok, partner?" she asked her darkling companion.

He and Tiger phased out of visibility and reappeared beside her in a rush.

"I can barely contain myself," he told her slyly. "So I won't."

He dropped Tiger, kicked himself off the ground, and went half shadow. Like a missile, he shot upwards, crashing both into and through the very centre of the rock ceiling.

Horrific cracking, rumbling, scraping sounds shook the cave as the whole roof splintered and Jackson drilled upward until she could make out an opening to the world above, like a sky light. His process was so fast that he was back in front of her before she had registered it, and was stooping to lug Tiger back over one shoulder.

"In a minute, there'll be no cave or cave paintings for them to come back to," he announced, radiating with readiness.

"Oh God," she managed.

He was missing an awful lot of skin, scalp and hair, and apart from the shockingly white quality of his wild smile among the blood and dirt, more white bone was exposed in many places.

"No first class flight this time 'Miss Steel'," Jackson told her, sweeping her against himself with his free arm. "You fly shadow, you fly fast."

Loose rocks were falling around them and the cave was making even more alarming sounds now.

"You're going to fly us all the way back to base?" she gasped despite herself. "In this state it'll kill you."

"If I don't burn all this out of me right now," he said glowingly, "I'm dead anyway."

She realised that his heart was beating so hard and fast that she could feel it where she leaned. He was amped up, but she trusted him.

"Alright," she groaned. And she squeezed her eyes closed as she felt him pull her into shadows and tear her up from the solid ground.

Intangible or not, there was still enough of her mind left working for her to lose control of it and lose consciousness as they shot from the skylight and hurtled upward to penetrate the clouds.

| 17 |

Divine

She had fuzzy memories of the terrible speed of their journey. Of impossible visions of breaks in the clouds revealing snatches of land, sea and then land again. Of the burning heat as they had shot downward almost uncontrollably before Jackson must have reined them in.

There had been a terrible jolt as he had landed on his two materialising feet, still holding a reappearing Alley Cat and Tiger, on the roof of the National Museum.

Jackson had slumped down in a tangle of their bodies, and she had heard Edward's urgent voice as he had sensed them and arrived on the rooftop in moments.

Now she stretched out stiffly, frowning and blinking herself awake, and recognising that she was in the middle of The Curator's luxurious king bed. She wore one of his t-shirts, though nothing else, and felt supremely well rested.

The curtains were drawn and the lighting was dim, but she could make out the figure laid out on the chaise near the window.

Swinging her legs out from under the covers, she silently padded from the bed to the chaise, gazing down at him to assess the damage.

The blood had been cleaned away and his tattered shirt had been removed, though he had been left un-bandaged. There were large bruises in the centre of his chest and down his ribs, but all of the missing skin had returned – with only raw, scar-like marks where before there had been devastating chasms. Traces of dark veins still stood out on his pale skin, along with shadows under his eyes. But otherwise, Jackson was back to being extremely dashing.

"That was exhilarating," she heard him murmur, and she noticed him peering up at her through half closed lashes and with a quirk to his lips.

"At least you didn't die," she answered sardonically. "Marcus said an OD like that would be permanent, and I'm sure Edward would never have forgiven me."

"I feel very much alive," he reassured her, and reached out to wrap his hand around the back of her thigh with a lazily widening smile.

"You were high," Alley Cat pointed out. "Probably still are."

"Probably." He pulled her closer while moving his hand upward. "Tsk tsk," he whispered. "No underwear."

"The Curator most likely didn't have my size," she answered, shivering pleasantly as his hand kept travelling up her back, along her ribs, and across to take advantage of The Curator not having her bra size either. "Your touch is still burning," she commented.

"I'm burning up all over," he agreed in a velvety voice, and seemed pleased when she reached down to place a hand on his chest.

"Your heart is still racing."

"I should think so," he smirked, and trailed his hand back down and then up between her thighs. His fingers were certain in their movements.

First stroking their way over her most sensitive yet explosive bud, and then pushing up and in to rub a deeper, more sensual point.

Alley Cat felt sparks of pleasure beginning to ebb upward – bursting in her stomach, tingling in her wrists, and heating up her cheeks.

"Jackson," Edward's voice came from the shadows at the doorway. "You realise you died yesterday."

Alley Cat blinked, realising she was gripping the back of the chaise with one hand and now leaning her weight on Jackson's chest with her other.

Jackson did not stop his motions. Gazing up at her evilly.

"Your twin killed me. But you brought me back, my friend," Jackson told Edward quietly. "That was quite the kiss of life."

"You … did die?" Alley Cat breathed.

"A true death. I never thought I would have to resuscitate a darkling," Edward glowered, and in a sudden haze, he had appeared quite solidly behind Alley Cat. Standing so close she could feel him. He put his hands on her hips as if to draw her back from Jackson. "You both nearly died from that journey."

"And yet," Jackson drawled. "Only I got the kiss of life. Now it's her turn."

Alley Cat was struggling to stand up without shaking, her

legs were quivering beneath her as the pin-pricks of passion travelled from Jackson's motions to spread all through her body.

"Did I ever tell you," Jackson went on, talking to Alley Cat. "That Edward and I make a great team?"

She heard a sigh of exasperation from behind her.

"Just ask Charlotte. And Jocelyn," Jackson advised.

"Jocelyn," Edward murmured with a tone of craving and sadness. But Alley Cat felt Edward's large hands move from her hips to the hem of her shirt. He drew it up, his touch intentionally brushing along her body, before he lifted it over her head.

"See Edward. No underwear," Jackson grinned. "Had no choice."

"I see," Edward agreed slowly. "Well if you want to do this, you best get up."

Edward wrapped one strong, dark arm around Alley Cat's waist from behind, and pressing against her, he leaned forward to grip Jackson's forearm – pulling his friend upright. Then Edward half phased, half physically dragged them all backward to the bed.

Breathlessly, Alley Cat found herself lying back against Edward's now bare, muscular torso, with Jackson kneeling on the floor at the foot of the bed.

Edward ran his fingers down her arms – taking hold of her wrists and lifting them back so she could rest her hands on either side of his neck. In turn, he began to kiss down her neck.

Simultaneously Jackson ran his hands from her inner thigh to her knees and ankles – leaving trails of fire as he drew her legs apart. Jackson's eyes were smouldering as he leaned forward over her. And then Jackson was kissing between her thighs.

She groaned as Jackson's tongue languidly moved over the small pearl that his fingers had inflamed earlier – each stroke like the stoking of a growing ember. She arched back into Edward as his arm held her to his smooth skin and as his fingers roamed from one nipple to the other.

"We make a good team because we want our lovers to be satisfied." Edward's full lips were like magic against her ear, neck and shoulder. It felt like time was blurring. "We will search for what works for you. For as long as it takes."

Alley Cat's eyelashes were fluttering. "This is working," she groaned.

Jackson growled against her, sending vibrations right through her core.

"Not just a quick fix," Edward disagreed. "We want deep, true gratification. That takes time to build. She's too close Jax, switch it up."

Alley Cat gasped as Edward eased her up and slipped out from underneath her, lowering her against the mattress so he could lean beside her. At the same time, Jackson pulled her closer to the end of the bed and stopped the caresses of his tongue, instead sucking at and kissing her pleasure point – creating a new sensation that made her moan as the ember inside her grew even brighter and warmer.

Edward brushed her hair from her eyes and cupped her face in a large palm. He held her gaze as she gripped onto his wrist, trying to stay focused on him as he obviously regarded her.

"You won me over when I realised that you had saved Jax," Edward told her. "Not just by saving him from what your friend Tiger was doing. But by making him come alive again. Maybe you will help us to save Jocelyn too."

Edward angled her face to his, and slowly, with heated intensity, pressed his magic lips against hers – his own tongue mirroring what Jackson's was doing elsewhere, with as much passion and electricity.

Alley Cat was unable to respond beyond a gasp when he broke from the kiss and trailed his plush lips over her collarbone and stomach.

"Change it up," she heard Edward say. "Make her feel it."

And then Jackson's tongue had trailed down from her first pleasure point, and was entering her like a spear before hooking in search of her inner, buzzing zone.

She cried out, her feet arching and her fingers grasping at the sheets and at Edward's muscled back while Edward reached down to stroke the throbbing bud that Jackson's attention had left. Edward kissed her again – long and slow and with feeling.

Jackson's insistent tongue was driving her to an edge. The ember had grown to a flame and was nearing a moment of explosive proportions.

"What do you want?" Edward whispered when he drew back.

"More ..." she was struggling to keep a grip. "More of you."

Jackson withdrew from where he was. Even in the dim light she could still see the shadows under his eyes and the bruises across his kneeling body. "You heard the woman," he told Edward, his gaze devouring her as he reached over her body and pulled her up by her arms.

Jackson drew her to himself at the foot of the bed so that she was up on her knees before him, and he circled her arms around his neck so that she had to lean forward – resting her forehead on his shoulder.

Edward was behind her, his skin on her skin, and his hands massaging her back.

Jackson reached through Alley Cat's parted legs to take hold of Edward, guiding him closer and pulling him into position. It was Edward's turn to groan from the firm pressure of Jackson's grip as he slowly eased Edward into the very tender, primed place that Jackson had himself prepared so well.

"Follow my lead," Jackson almost purred to Edward, and he began to massage Alley Cat with his fingers again, while Edward followed the sensual rhythm with full, internal movements – pressing in and savouring each sensation.

Alley Cat's breaths matched their timing as she held onto Jackson and felt her core now rolling with slowly building, electrified magma. Each thrust filled and overflowed her.

Time wasn't the only thing melting now. She was.

And the slow build of pace as both Jackson and Edward worked together made every inch of her feel as if it needed to scream.

The rubbing motion of one, and the hard, insistent pushing motion of the other overwhelmed her mind until she could hardly think but of the constant movements inside and over her.

Then rather than a frenzied explosion, the flames that had been building inside of her simply grew to such intensity that they rolled into one ground shaking release of breaking waves that swept through them all.

She gasped into Jackson's neck and clung to him while Edward curved over her, moving in sync with her tense, helpless waves of ecstasy. Pressing into her, and pressing her into himself, before finally breathing hard against her back and hugging her to himself – relaxing against her intimately.

It was only when Jackson sank down to sprawl on the rug at the base of the bed, grinning up at them both impishly but tiredly, that Edward gently retreated from her.

Edward pulled Alley Cat backward to lie against the pillows and shifted the covers to smooth them over her. Then, in his glorious nakedness, he leant over and pulled Jackson up, supporting and forcing him over to join Alley Cat under the covers. Finally Edward slid in on Alley Cat's other side, and she was warmed by the touch of the two strong, silky bodies against her.

"Go to sleep," Edward instructed Jackson, leaning up on his elbow and reaching over to smooth Jackson's brow.

"Who gives the orders around here?" Jackson argued, closing his eyes obediently.

"You do," Edward smiled.

"Right you are," Jackson sighed. "I'm going to sleep."

| 18 |

Contemplation

Alley Cat woke to the comforting weight of Edward's arm over her chest, and the warmth of Jackson leaning against her back.

Edward's face was close to hers and he slowly blinked awake when he felt her gaze on him.

"Morning," he murmured quietly.

"You surprise me," Alley Cat told him just as quietly. "I did not guess you would so easily change your mind about me."

"Never fear," Edward gave a slight smile. "I'm not your best friend. But getting Jax out of there was an impressive feat – and I feel responsible for CARE meddling with us at all."

"You are very close to Jackson, I understand your protectiveness over him."

Edward raised himself up onto his elbow, sighing. "There are others of us around the world. Not many. But Charlotte and Jackson found me when I was first born, and we spent many decades together. They are my family."

"How did Jocelyn come to be part of that family?" Alley Cat asked softly.

At the mention of Jocelyn a flicker of pain crossed Edward's dark brow.

"Jocelyn originally came in search of Jackson, as they all do at different times. And when Charlotte, Jackson and I helped her, I became enamoured. I couldn't leave her when all was done. We stayed together for many lifetimes and have re-entered each other's lives many times. For darklings, we are as close as it comes to what humans call 'married'. No matter our time wandering apart, we are each other's."

Alley Cat was quiet for a moment, thinking. "Why do they always come to Jackson, as you say?" she asked then with a frown.

"He was the first of us," Edward answered. "He was born from the first truly evil deeds and intentions of mankind, and he set the precedent for darklings. He wandered for a long time alone, learning to be what he was. It was some time before other darklings began to appear, and he helped each of us to learn and to adapt too."

"He was a mentor?"

"Oh he didn't want to be," Edward smiled. "He just wanted to help us get on our feet and then be on his way. But we are all drawn to him, and he can never shake us for long."

"He is quite charismatic," Alley Cat agreed.

"And fun," Edward added. "But he also always seems to know what to do. Calm and instinctual. Like when Jocelyn came to him for help." Edward closed his eyes, remembering his meeting with her. "We had been in China, which was doing quite well when Rome fell, and we had decided we would take a break from the action. But Jocelyn left Britain to find us, desperate for help to contain the levels of barbarous, ignorant malice spreading through the 'Dark Ages'. She had been the only one in Europe at the time, and while it normally only takes a couple of darklings per continent to prowl around and skim the darkness from the population – moderating flare ups in problem areas, this time it took all four of us. Four darklings to come close to maintaining the level of selfishness and suspicion festering in people at that time. We were complete gluttons for that entire era."

"Every day was a feast," Jackson's drowsy voice announced. He snaked his arm around Alley Cat's stomach and pulled her closer against himself. "A party. For us at least."

"Though even that time didn't come close to nearly killing us with overdoses," Edward remarked dryly.

"Neither did the astronomical levels of hate and bloodlust of the World Wars." Jackson's breath tickled Alley Cat's spine. "What your counterpart, Mister Marcus Knight, did to Tiger was not normal or human. Even extreme rage and loathing is human, but that was something else. Unnatural."

"Why don't more darklings keep appearing for each terrible time in history?" Alley Cat questioned curiously.

"Oh, we think they would appear if they were needed," Edward mused. "To help humanity maintain balance without being overwhelmed by the bad. But there has always been enough of us spread out to keep on top of things normally. Or enough of us to find Jax and be banded together under his lead if we needed a more unified front."

"Find Jax," Jackson muttered, using the tone of one who is

rolling their eyes. "Even though darklings can just watch the news and know where to go for themselves these days."

"Find Jax," Edward agreed with a grin. "Because he can't help but come up with a game plan that others will listen to."

"Even though he just wants to be left alone," Jackson lamented.

"Well," Edward stretched. "I might leave you alone then."

"Go find us some nice clothes," Jackson instructed. "We can't go out like this. As nice as we look."

"Of course, my friend," Edward grinned, and then leaned forward to press his lips to Alley Cat's before sliding out of bed.

"You'd be a laughing stock," Edward went on. "And I need you to be serious. There's much to discuss for us to go forward." He was already zipping up his trousers and pulling on his shirt.

Alley Cat was shaking her head as Edward left and Jackson trailed his fingers up and down her arm. "He is a tough man to figure out," she remarked.

"Hardly a man," Jackson teased. "But he was just jealous before we let him share in the fun."

"Hmm," Alley Cat was unconvinced.

"Plus all those things he said last night," Jackson sobered up a little, and pulled her to face him. "You were instrumental in me escaping an oddly powerful new opponent. Something we've never seen before. Something fatal. Something that has Jocelyn." He reached up to tuck her hair behind her ear. "So he may not be your 'best friend' yet – but he cares for and finds hope in you."

"Just how much of our conversation did you listen to?" Alley Cat cocked a sarcastic eyebrow.

"If you insist on talking where I'm trying to sleep, then I insist on listening," he assured her languidly.

"Alright then, reluctant mentor of the darklings, and sleep deprived victim of this bed –" she pulled the sheets down from his bruised chest and lifted herself up to lay on him. "Continue to educate me as Edward was. Tell me more."

"Oh cat of the night, lady assassin of my dreams," Jackson replied. "What might you desire to know?"

She rested her chin on her hands, which were folded over his heart. "I'll start easy. What is it like to be born a darkling?"

"Easy question," Jackson agreed. "We just appear."

"Please go on."

He rubbed at his still dark eyes. "I appeared in Africa. I was just suddenly manifesting – energy pulling itself together and sparking into a conscious being. Though it's hazy, I remember I was adult-sized, but so ignorant as to be vulnerable. Not understanding that I was different, or what I was or why."

Jackson's chest rose and fell with a deep breath, and Alley Cat noticed that his heart had slowed to a normal rate.

"The first creatures were primitive things, but I am quite sure I was born when one of those creatures killed another for more than just survival reasons. It was likely the first time a hominid killed another to gain some kind of power or advantage." He brushed his knuckles over her cheekbone. "I left to spend much of my early days feeding off ancient hunter-gatherers between far north and far south Europe. I evolved greatly in those parts."

"That explains the pale complexion," Alley Cat nodded.

"But," Jackson went on, "while I looked like those first people, it was very clear that I was separate and alone. At the start I accidentally drained people to death just by trying to be near them for comfort. And I fast learned that being different was dangerous, and kept to myself when I could. It was only after a great span of time, when larger groups had left Africa for places like Europe as I said, that other darklings began popping up in the world. It was so that there were enough to cover the new populations developing. Charlotte appeared in what would now be Scotland. Others appeared around the Americas and Australia. Jocelyn was in the Mediterranean. Edward was back in the heart of Africa." Jackson stopped there and chuckled. "Is the next question as 'easy'?"

"I want to know what you think can be done about Tiger," she replied, and now Jackson winced.

"Not so simple," he said honestly. "The darkness was rolling off of him when he attacked me. I couldn't help but absorb it, and it did slow him down. However, taking more darkness won't fix him, and putting the darkness back would of course be a bad move – we'll be back to square one."

"So you think he needs a different kind of energy dose," Alley Cat asserted gravely.

Jackson nodded. "Somehow, he needs the light put back in him."

"And last question," Alley Cat moved on from an impossible topic.

"Here we go," Jackson steeled himself.

"Where do the two of us stand?" she asked bluntly. "Seeing as we both enjoy each other, but prefer to be alone."

"Ahhh," he rolled the word gleefully. "Remember me saying some people taste like sweet, sugary lies? Or strawberry innocence? Or oily greed?" he took a deep breath as if catching the aroma of a fine wine. "You taste like freshly sliced oranges dipped in dark chocolate coating. Your direct honesty is scrumptious."

"I'm not after anything long term in the traditional sense," she continued, un-phased. "Especially not as long term as you're capable of."

He snickered. "Just imagine you wheeling into your nursing home bedroom to find me waiting on your bed. The perfect surprise."

"In my line of work I shouldn't live that long," Alley Cat answered flatly.

"Well then," he considered his answer – a playful glint still in his eyes. "Based on your potential life span, our romance will be a whirlwind one to me. Short, but extremely enjoyable. I might not always be with you, but part of the game can be you catching and killing me every time I hunt you down."

"It could be fun," she said. "You're a loner until you want to visit, and I kill you off when I don't want to be tied down," she shrugged. "But you can't get jealous if you blow into town and I'm busy or playing with somebody else."

"I'll know that a part of you is always mine," he told her. "And jealousy just heightens the passion."

Alley Cat sat up as Edward re-entered the room with an arm full of designer shopping bags.

"Jackson's kind of jealousy is famous," Edward announced, setting the bags out at the foot of the bed. "But he just might become a constant highlight in your life for as long as you live."

"Or if it doesn't work," Jackson beamed brightly, "I can just darken your pretty, precious mind."

Jackson grabbed her by the wrist and hauled her up and out of bed.

"Coming?" he asked Edward, as he led the way to a side door entering a bathroom.

"I'm too tired," Edward answered blandly. "As you should be. And The Curator is getting impatient."

"We'll be out in an hour," Jackson informed him, already closing the bathroom door.

| 19 |

Game Plan

He started by soaping every inch of her, and ended up behind her, his hand between her legs. Her own hands were splayed over the wet wall tiles as she was gripped by his attentions – breathing hard in a shroud of steam and falling water.

Finally, when the pulsing and rushing of her blood had ebbed, she leaned her head back on his shoulder and felt him kiss her neck.

"Being stalked by you for the rest of my life might be just what I need," she told him with a husk in her voice and a tone of satisfaction.

"Let's hope we both get to live to see how this plays out," Jackson smiled as she turned to run the soap across his torso and circled around to massage his shoulders.

"Your bruises are fading, and your skin looks slightly less grey," Alley Cat observed. "You're bouncing back from a proper death. So you might be ok."

"You're the only one to have successfully taken on a lightling," Jackson replied. "So I'm sure you'll be fine too."

Then he sighed and leaned forward to shut the water off, stepping out and selecting a towel to wrap her in before he began to dry himself.

"This is the first time in a long time that we have faced something so new," he mused soberly. "And it is the first time in all of time that we have faced opponents that are even remotely similar to us." He pushed back his wet hair and led her from the bathroom to the bags that Edward had brought. "We've always just gone along for the ride with whatever was happening to people at each phase of history."

"Times change. So must you," Alley Cat shrugged, sliding into the under garments Edward had selected.

"Oh my lord," Jackson whistled. "He chose a sheer lingerie set for you, and expected we could just get dressed in a rush?"

"Yes," she smirked. "We've got to surface from this room and face things."

He bit his knuckle and turned from her to focus on dressing himself in a crisp shirt and trousers. Then he followed when she was ready to re-join the real world beyond the bedroom door.

"Only forty minutes," Edward greeted them from the massive screen desk at the centre of The Curator's large office. "Very well restrained, Jackson."

"You'll have to change the sheets," Jackson told The Curator pleasantly. "And the shower."

The Curator scowled, wheeling himself over to where Edward waited – sets of blue prints on the screen, analysis equipment and Alley Cat's scanner and test tube from the cave ready in front of them.

"Alley Cat," The Curator made an effort to assume an

unbothered countenance. "You managed to photograph and arrange data on your scanner. But we would appreciate your expert eye to guide us in analysing what's going on, and what makes these pictures so important that we had to race CARE to get them."

Alley Cat and Jackson joined them, taking seats on the opposite side of the table. She unscrewed the lid of the test tube and let the little painted sample out onto a petri dish, before hovering her scanner over the small rock shard.

"Last time Tiger and I went through a carbon dating process as we got into those unexplored, secret caves," Alley Cat began, carefully reading the data that her scanner was returning. "Those deeper caves are of course ancient. But according to this, so is the clay based paint that was used for the cave art. Whoever painted it was there when the first people were, but with the skills of a modern human."

"Which lines up with what Marcus Knight said," Jackson nodded, folding his hands on the table top comfortably. "He seemed to think that my counterpart – 'Mister White', was the artist. And if I was the first darkling, surely Mister White was the first lightling."

"Were you painting masterpieces when you first materialised?" The Curator asked Jackson with a raised brow.

Jackson chuckled. "Hardly. But I suppose we took on our own traits, characteristic of the creature we each became. While I was out being hungry and sucking up as much darkness as I could, he was probably off spreading goodness and peace. Or creating fine art. Hippy."

Using the tabletop screen Alley Cat logged into the files

that she'd sent herself from the cave. She projected the images that opened up onto all of the screens around the room.

"This is the first image, or the image that was central in the cave. The others flowed from it and the scanner recognised it as the start of the story that was being told," Alley Cat explained. "You can see two man-like figures, or early people. Look at their broad brows and stocky build."

The two primitive men were locked in battle, though one figure was clearly losing, with the other pinning him down and holding a rock in one fist. Ready to commit murder.

"I think we're seeing my birth," Jackson commented blithely.

"I would agree," Alley Cat told him. "Can you see the faint circles surrounding both of the figures?"

"They're similar to the halos of light that normally get painted on images of the Madonna with her babe," The Curator observed with interest.

"Though their halos are most often just around the heads of the Madonna and child," Edward added, leaning closer. "These circles go all the way around each man."

"We can guess that rather than these circles being a symbol of divinity, they in fact represent each man's spirit," Alley Cat mused. "Because look at what happens in the next image."

She swiped to the next painting and now there was a lifeless victim with no circle at all, and the victorious man was standing beside him. However, the victorious man's circle was split in two and rising away from him – as if it had become untethered from the person it was supposed to be attached to.

With another flick there was a new painting in the sequence, and this time the two separating parts of the circle each showed the surfacing image of two faces that were identical to the face of the victorious, murderous man below.

"Thankfully, evolution has been kind to me," Jackson mused, eyeing off his origin story warily. "That is not a flattering baby picture."

"I can see the likeness," The Curator replied.

"Did I mention your bedsheets?" Jackson chimed. "I'm getting tired again."

"After this we are shown the two circles drifting apart and becoming more distinct, physical beings," Alley Cat continued with interest. "So it's like that first, terrible act split the soul of the world's first murderer. His soul was shattered into good and bad sides, which took on lives of their own."

"One appears to be off terrorising and leaching energy from groups of people," Edward pointed out. "That one has been drawn with a rather monstrous expression."

"That one would be me," Jackson coughed. "Who knew realism started so early in art?"

"The other appears to be trying to join and heal people," Edward added.

"The lines around both figures show us the direction of their energies," The Curator noted. "The direction of the lines drawn around the monster one are painted to be coming from the groups of people and into himself. And he seems strong. The healing one is sending lines out of himself and into the people, but he seems fragile."

"It's all in the name," Jackson steepled his fingers. "Lightling gives light, darkling takes dark." He leaned back as Alley Cat swiped to the next image, which showed the state of affairs worsening for the fragile healing figure that was one day to become Mister White.

The painting showed the monstrous version of Jackson among groups of early people. He had become taller and healthier, and the groups of humans were all chaotic, argumentative and disorganised.

On the other hand, the future Mister White had collapsed, but was reaching out to the primitive people desperately, while the few lines he had left to send out appeared to be too weak to penetrate them.

The last image was of Mister White by himself in a dark cave. He was small and sickly, and huddling sadly in the overpowering shadows.

"Always knew I was a villain," Jackson broke the silence. "Apparently I helped to spread sin and corruption for my own selfish appetite."

Alley Cat shook her head. "That doesn't make sense," she disagreed. "As you said yourself, you absorb darkness rather than spread it. Perhaps people just gave you plenty to feed off."

"The lightling does appear to be unable to keep up with his own purpose. Giving goodness from himself exhausted him and he couldn't keep up," The Curator acquiesced. "If the darklings hadn't appeared to moderate and drain the levels of darkness building in humanity as we struggled to survive, who knows what the world would be like."

Edward rubbed his furrowed brow in consternation. "Why wouldn't they want us to know that they spread goodness? Or to see these paintings?" he sat forward. "These paintings prove that violence is unnatural to the point that it splits and shatters a person. And they prove that lightlings are good. They literally put the goodness in people. Isn't that a message they would be happy with?"

"The paintings also show lightlings as inhuman, and as overwhelmed. He gave up," Alley Cat tapped her chin thoughtfully. "But worse – the paintings tell us that a lightling's job is to get weak, to give themselves up for the benefit of others. Would you say that CARE does either of those things?"

Jackson winced and rubbed at his chest, where Tiger had pummelled him. "They sure got strong somehow. And they sure have brainwashed followers that lack a lot of goodness."

"Perhaps they're taking goodness from people, to get stronger themselves?" The Curator grimaced.

"I'd probably track down and destroy those paintings too, if that were me," Alley Cat said.

Edward's shoulders slumped. "So now they are messing with darklings, making contact with me and … taking Jocelyn … because …" his jaw clenched. "They must have reached a stage where they are ready to study their opponents. Where they'll decide if we are useful to them, or a threat."

Jackson grunted, but there was a trace of concern in his expression. "What did you two learn about CARE and how to rescue Jocelyn while we were away?" he asked The Curator and Edward.

The Curator pinched the bridge of his nose tiredly. "We studied every nook and cranny of their complex. We created virtual tours through the place, based on these blue prints and Alley Cat's information. We have memorised where every corner, every garbage bin and every framed certificate is situated. So we can find our way around the place –"

"But?" Jackson cocked an eyebrow.

"But we found no way in," Edward grimaced in frustration. "CARE dominate the field of technology and hoard their best inventions for themselves. Their security is impenetrable. We can't get in without someone helping us from the inside."

"Then perhaps we need someone back on the inside," Alley Cat answered, crossing her arms.

"No," Jackson and The Curator answered at once.

"I was recently offered a job by Mister Marcus Knight, Vice President himself," Alley Cat reminded Jackson.

"That was before you cut his heart out and we collapsed a cave on him," Jackson reminded her in return.

"They're going to come for us soon anyway," Alley Cat declared. "They can't let us keep Tiger, who is evidence of what they're doing. Or these images, and what they have taught us."

"Nobody in the world would believe what we have learned," Edward said a little doubtfully.

"Nobody?" Alley Cat questioned. "The world is a big place, and CARE surely has as many enemies as allies. Plus, CARE have no idea what the darklings are willing to do to expose their lightling persecutors."

"Then you suggest we just hand you over?" The Curator asked.

"I suggest we get a message to them, that we want them to help Tiger and release Jocelyn. And that I will work for them in exchange."

"Still no," Jackson replied in a testy tone.

"I'm not a darkling, darling," she smouldered at him. "Your words are not gospel."

"They're definitely not gospel," Jackson retorted. "But do you really expect that they'll trust you to just walk in and work with them?"

"Of course not," she smiled. "They'll suck me dry and try to attack and hurt all of you too. But I'll be in, and you'll have to figure out a way to cure me."

"I think we best develop this plan some more," The Curator suggested, reaching for the coffee jug. "Before they work out where we're based."

| 20 |

Pleasure

Edward finished the last dregs of his third coffee and The Curator was nodding to himself broodingly, his normally neat, greying hair now mussed.

Alley Cat stretched and pushed herself back from the table. "We'll get the ball rolling and reach out to them tomorrow. In the meantime," she crossed toward a door at the far end of the office, "I'm going down to visit Tiger."

"We'll join you," Jackson told her sweetly, rising with Edward. "And then adjourn to my place so that our dear Curator may have his bed back."

The Curator straightened in his wheelchair. "I'm probably better off staying in the chair and burning the bed. But I'll be glad to be rid of you for the night." He waved them off and they followed Alley Cat from the room.

"This is the restoration wing," Alley Cat informed them. There were a few museum staff members packing their tools away and winding up their projects for the evening. "Tiger will be down in the cellars. We don't usually store anything of value there – just packaged food and bottled water for emergencies. But it has been reinforced in case of times such as this."

"The Curator just thinks of everything, doesn't he?" Jackson drawled.

"He actually does," Alley Cat nodded. "He has secret walls through all of the levels, with passages that pop out at key sections and exits of the museum. But most importantly, he has each irreplaceable item in his galleries on climate controlled, sealable shelves or podiums. In a second, each treasure can be enclosed in a chamber so air tight that any threat is rendered useless."

"You can't deny he cares about his vocation," Edward replied. "And I admit he is quite brilliant, after working with him while you were away."

"Through here," Alley Cat had turned them into a clearly little used corridor, and down a ramp. At the bottom she switched on the dim lights and gestured to a very modern door set in highly updated, and out of place cellar walls. They were all heavily reinforced.

She crossed to key in a code on the panel at the door. "Now stay put. I just need to see him, and listen for if Tiger is still anywhere in there," she explained. "I don't need you two coming in and dying on me."

"We'll stay perfectly behaved in the doorway," Jackson raised placating hands.

She pushed the door open quickly, stepping into the room fearlessly. As promised, Edward and Jackson simply stood shoulder to shoulder, blocking the doorway.

"Ohhh, A – Ceeee," came Tiger's low growl. "Glad you haven't forgotten me, girl."

Tiger was seated on a bunker style cot against the far wall. His posture was totally upright and stiff, not matching his friendly tone at all.

"How you doing, Tige?" Alley Cat asked, just as nicely.

Tiger cocked his head to the side, his completely dark eyes still managing to glint with energy. "Been better A.C. I mean, look where helping you got me. Locked up in a musty cellar with tins of tuna and beans."

"I'm sorry that you're involved in all this. I never wanted anything to happen to you," Alley Cat told him seriously.

"Well the way I see it," Tiger stood slowly. "Anything did happen to me. But they'd been tracking me for my own sake for months." He stepped forward. "My real problem with it is you locking me up like an animal – after all I've done for you. The rest of it I'm pretty happy about."

"Happy?" Alley Cat questioned, circling around to his side.

"Ecstatic," Tiger amended. "Liberated. My inhibitions are gone."

"We'll get you back to normal," Alley Cat promised him. "You'll remember that you like being mostly made of goodness."

In the blink of an eye, Tiger rushed at Alley Cat and shoved her against the wall, leaning one arm against her throat to keep her trapped. Alley Cat shot both Edward and Jackson a glare over Tiger's shoulder that stopped them in their tracks, and they fell back to wait like surly children.

"You won't get them away from the door that easily," she scolded Tiger, and Edward fast became sheepish rather than surly as he realised how quickly that had nearly worked. Jackson simply glowered.

"Maybe I don't care about them," Tiger stated slowly, bringing his face close to hers. "I could kill them both with a touch. That's why you're keeping them over there."

"You're sure?" Alley Cat quirked an eyebrow. "You think you could kill them both, without damaging yourself?"

Tiger smirked. "Dunno about no damage to myself. But, no inhibitions, remember?"

Then he forced a heated kiss to her lips, gripping her face and crushing her against the wall until she hurled a fist into his throat and he dropped – stunned and rasping horribly.

"No inhibitions," she agreed. "You never would have tried that before."

He clutched his gullet and stared blankly up at her as she circled back around him and to the doorway.

"I will find a way to get my friend back," she assured him. "But in the meantime, consider how no inhibitions can be dangerous."

Edward and Jackson backed out of the doorway to let her pass.

"Are you alright?" Edward asked as she sealed the door again.

"I've spent a great deal of time hunting down the worst people on this planet to cull CARE's allies," Alley Cat replied. "I've dealt with worse than a stolen kiss."

"It's different when it's your own friend," Edward shook his head. "That couldn't have been pleasant."

"Speaking of unpleasantness and the worst people on the planet," Jackson changed the topic, "let's visit Charlotte's Bar."

"The red head," Alley Cat grinned.

"We're becoming regulars," Edward commented. "She'll start to charge."

"We're bringing the murderess with us this time," Jackson countered. "Surely that'll prevent any mess or trouble."

Security waved them past the long line that had already formed when they arrived, and Charlotte's face lit up when she saw them enter. She slid off the polished countertop of the bar, where she had been lounging like a fiery burlesque queen.

"You're alive!" she cried out, flinging her arms around Jackson's neck and drawing Edward in too.

"Mostly," Jackson agreed, kissing her cheekbone. "Evening, Mick," he added in greeting for Charlotte's hulking man-servant.

"What are you doing about Jocelyn?" Charlotte demanded, now herding them toward her private office. "Should I call the others?"

"Keep your pretty head out of the firing line," Jackson told her, taking a seat in her favourite armchair and pulling her over to sit on his lap.

"We're not sure if sending out calls for help will just give CARE a bunch of red flags for where all the darklings are spread around the world," Edward explained.

"But they deserve to know to be wary. They deserve to know about Jocelyn," Charlotte asserted. "Can't you do it like you did in the old days? A call to arms?" she asked Jackson then. "We've always come when you've called."

"That was before land, sea and sky were so easily observed," Jackson mused, tracing a lock of red hair that ran down her shoulder and over her breast. "But I don't think they can trace us travelling in shadow form, it's more by the patterns of people's behaviour around us, and by phone calls."

"Should I go?" Charlotte asked. "I can put them all on alert at least. Mick can run this place."

Mick grunted in affirmation.

"Go tomorrow then," Jackson sighed. "As under the radar as you can possibly be."

"That's settled," Charlotte agreed with a nod. "Now, to my next topic." Her focus switched to Alley Cat, who was leaning against the desk. "You brought a friend."

"I'm not sure that Sherice and some of your other girls would agree with that title," Jackson grinned. "Alley Cat didn't give off friendly vibes when she was last here."

"A lifetime ago," Alley Cat shrugged.

"It's nice to meet you properly," Charlotte told Alley Cat.

"Likewise," Alley Cat nodded.

Charlotte disappeared from Jackson's lap and materialised beside Alley Cat. "Do you have a safe place to stay tonight?" she asked the murderess.

"With me," Jackson demurred.

"You can stay in my dungeon instead," Charlotte told Alley Cat sweetly.

Edward rolled his eyes. "You thought Jackson's was a safe enough place for me to stay at."

"Maybe I want a night of protection for myself," Charlotte fluttered her eyelashes.

"You have Mick," Jackson protested.

"The dungeon sounds interesting," Alley Cat cut in.

"Oh it is! Shall I take you down and show you?" Charlotte was beaming brightly.

"It's just a mood-lit bedroom with black velvet walls," Edward objected.

"The specialty bed in your dungeon is big enough for all of us," Jackson gave in. "Alley Cat stays, so do we."

"Oh I wouldn't have it any other way," Charlotte declared. "We make such a great team. But let's have a drink or two first."

Charlotte ushered them all out into the club, where the music was now pumping with such vibrations that the sound was a physical force.

Dancers on the front podiums undulated their hips and rotated their bodies, hands roaming over their own skin. Crowds full of heat and intense desire pressed in around them and pulsed with the music in waves.

Charlotte's eyes were glimmering and she flashed a cheeky smile as she took hold of Alley Cat's wrist and let herself be absorbed into the thronging masses – forcing Alley Cat to follow and to get lost in the people rather than searching for the bar.

Charlotte drew Alley Cat into the centre of things, and as the lights in the club pulsated and a sea of limbs moved to the throbbing sound, they couldn't help but move together too. Dancing so close, so in rhythm with each other, that it was like they were making love already.

Charlotte threw her head back and laughed, revelling in the energy that poured into her from the dance floor. Alley Cat pulled the fiery darkling close and kissed her neck, holding torrents of flaming hair back from Charlotte's shoulders and then kissing up Charlotte's jaw and behind her ear.

Charlotte swayed against Alley Cat, pressing in against her and moving so that now both their hips and their lips met – hot and hard and insistent.

Alley Cat sucked at and then bit on Charlotte's lower lip, roving her hands down Charlotte's shoulders, back and the curve of her behind so that their hips were grinding tightly – slowly and simultaneously.

Alley Cat began to move her fingers lower, under the hem of Charlotte's party dress. She traced her touch over the damp material between Charlotte's legs. At the same time, Charlotte was at the right height to begin pressing sensual kisses to Alley Cat's collarbones, her lips sweet and plush as they trailed over Alley Cat's skin.

"Miss Charlotte?"

Silken hair brushed against Alley Cat and Charlotte's cheeks as a blonde woman fought to be close enough to them to be heard. The blonde woman had put her hand on Charlotte's arm to get the darkling's attention, but had frozen when her eyes had picked up Alley Cat's features in the flashing lights.

"What is it Sherice?" Charlotte called back.

"Jax ... Mister Flint says to tell you ..." Sherice swallowed. "That he's bored."

"How could he be bored, speaking to you my little Sherry?" Charlotte laughed, still holding Alley Cat close with her hand pressing on the back of the murderess' thigh. "You're dazzling."

"Your jewels are spectacular," Alley Cat added. Because jewellery was all that Sherice was wearing tonight.

"Tha … thank you," Sherice swallowed, still eyeing Alley Cat warily over her shoulder as Charlotte shooed her away.

Both Alley Cat and Charlotte were flushed as if feverish when they broke from the crushing waves of people and made it to the corner of the bar where Edward and Jackson waited.

Jackson was leaning back against the bar, glaring at Charlotte. "You're greedy."

"Of course!" Charlotte giggled. "Self-indulgence is what I do."

Edward gestured to four lines of shots, ready and waiting on the bar, and the three darklings raised their glasses to throw back the first shots of fiery liquid – the alcohol lighting flames in their eyes almost immediately.

There were clinks as row after row of shot glasses were slung back.

"Not thirsty?" Charlotte asked Alley Cat, taking up an untouched glass.

"I rarely drink," Alley Cat replied, grabbing a water instead. "Especially not when I have work tomorrow. I make the right choices for my body."

"You clearly do," Charlotte replied, swiping another shot for herself. "So let me be one of those right choices."

With a devious grin, Charlotte pulled Alley Cat into a dim corner before turning them both shadow. Edward and Jackson followed suit, sweeping after them in shadow form.

Alley Cat dimly felt herself passing over the dance floor

like smoke, and then pouring down a hidden staircase, into what could only be Charlotte's own private quarters.

When she re-materialised, she found herself surrounded in the darklings, and near to the largest bed she'd ever seen.

"Wait 'til you see what Edward bought her," Jackson said, stepping forward and lifting Alley Cat's tank top up and over her head.

"Edward, you shouldn't have," Charlotte cried, reaching to rub the material of Alley Cat's sheer bra, as well as the pink, stiff skin visible beneath it. "How delicious."

"And matching underwear," Edward shrugged modestly. He grabbed the waistline of Alley Cat's pants and dragged her over so that he could unbutton and un-zip them. Jackson came from behind to draw them down her legs and turn them and her boots to shadow.

"A perfect set," Charlotte agreed, now hooking her finger-tips into a bra cup so that she could touch skin directly.

Edward traced a lingering touch over the fine, mesh between Alley Cat's legs, and Alley Cat took hold of Edward's face in front of her, leaning in to let her tongue flick over his.

She could taste the sharp remnants of alcohol as she kissed him forcefully, and she let her hands roam to his collar and then to his shirt buttons – undoing each of them to reveal dark, smooth muscles.

Jackson came to stand behind Edward, stripping the shirt back and away from him, and squeezing the tight muscles at the back of Edward's neck so that he groaned against Alley Cat's mouth.

Alley Cat gasped herself when Charlotte slipped her hand under the waist band and right down into Alley Cat's underwear. But Edward stifled Alley Cat's gasps with more fierce kisses.

Jackson pulled Edward back to sit against himself on the end of the bed – Alley Cat being drawn along too as the large darkling kept a hold of her waist. Then Jackson reached around to undo Edward's pants and to free Edward's straining length from his undergarments.

Charlotte released Alley Cat, and Alley Cat put her hands on Edward's thighs, pushing them open so that she could kneel down between them to continue her kissing there. Edward's head lolled back and Alley Cat's mouth was firm as she sucked on his impossible hardness, his veins pulsing with each lash of her tongue and tug of her lips.

Releasing his grip on Edward so that Alley Cat could properly take hold of the overcome darkling for herself, Jackson shadowed free of his own trousers, and reappeared behind Charlotte. Not hesitating, he literally tore the dress from Charlotte's body, ripped her underwear, and forced the straps of her bra down before unhooking it completely. He phased them both backward until Charlotte's spine was against a bed post, and before she'd even finished drawing her breath in she was moaning as he thrust into her, his hands cupping and pinching her pert, bouncing breasts.

Beside them Alley Cat climbed up to straddle Edward, pulling her sheer underwear aside and sinking onto his shaft so that his hardness now filled her totally. All she could feel was his breadth pushing in and then pulling out as she squeezed around him and moved up and down in his lap. She gripped his strong shoulders and pressed against his rippling stomach.

At the same time Charlotte groaned and ground herself against Jackson – her breasts bouncing with each push until he latched on to bite and suck at one of her nipples. They dragged against each other, biting and digging fingernails and pushing their hips against each other in a rolling rhythm until their release came in world shaking waves.

But when Jackson pressed hot kisses to her heaving chest, before unlatching himself to let her go, Charlotte grinned at him and then moved to stand behind Alley Cat – her breasts against Alley Cat's back as she fondled Alley Cat's own nipples in turn.

Jackson cocked an eyebrow to watch with desire as Charlotte's added sensations built Alley Cat to such an extreme climax, that as she seized and throbbed around him, Edward was overwhelmed himself.

Alley Cat's orgasmic pulses and dragging motions pulled at Edward until he was shuddering and spent, their cries and gasps only ending when Alley Cat's tense muscles relaxed around Edward's length so that they could all slump forward into each other, into Edward's arms as he sank back under the two women.

And they only stirred against Edward's chest when Jackson's movements drew their attention.

There was the sound of running water in an adjoining room, and Jackson returned to scoop up Charlotte and deposit her on the bed behind Edward. Then Jackson came to claim Alley Cat, drawing her up and off Edward so that Edward moaned again, lolling over to rest his shaven head on Charlotte's stomach.

"Enough sharing," Jackson told Alley Cat, standing her up in front of himself. "Now for our quality time."

He at last pulled her underwear down and off and then reached around her to unhook and discard her bra. Greedily, he brushed his hand over her breasts until her nipples stood up again, and then he shook his head and swept her up.

He carried her into a lavish bathroom, with an ornate, free standing bath tub. She sighed as he lowered her into the steam and running water, and then he stepped in behind her, cradling her back against himself.

"So far our quality time has seemed to involve you avoiding the ultimate connection with me," Alley Cat remarked. "You keep letting Edward do it."

Jackson leaned his chin on her shoulder and wrapped an arm around her middle. "When it's time for you and I to connect, it will be about you and I. Nobody and nothing else."

"Very well," she acquiesced, and reached back to hook her arm around his neck. "I look forward to it."

He took a handful of water and let it run out over her chest. "And it'll be worth it."

| 21 |

Action

Mick didn't bat an eye as he found the four of them entangled on the bed, waking them with coffee, fresh fruits and toast.

"Ohhhh," Charlotte moaned, her wrist over her eyes and Edward's head laying on her hip. "Did I really say I'd leave to shadow my way around the world?"

Jackson reached across from where he was sprawled out, with Alley Cat lounging on his chest. He traced his fingers over Charlotte's brow to move tendrils of hair to the side. "Only if you want to, Lottie."

Mick took Charlotte's wrist away from her eyes and pressed a coffee mug into her hand to inspire her to pull herself up.

"Mick will miss me so," Charlotte sighed, blowing on her coffee and reaching for a strawberry.

Mick grunted, but with a note of agreement. He left the room, returning with arms full of shopping bags. One each for Edward, Jackson and Alley Cat.

"You are indispensable," Jackson informed the man servant. "Mick is as well practiced at sizing people up and buying them a new wardrobe as Edward is," he explained to Alley Cat then. "Though his choices are a little more functional and a little less sexy than Edward's."

"Great," Alley Cat grinned, sitting up and selecting some grapes. "I could do with functional on an assignment day. Supportive bras are a necessity."

"Will you choose me something nice to travel in from the closet?" Charlotte yawned at Mick, and he obediently disappeared into a large side-room brimming with clothing. "The others would prefer a call to arms from Jackson himself," Charlotte explained to Alley Cat. "So the least I can do is look good for them."

"They know you and I are very close to Jax," Edward reassured her, rolling over and running his fingers over his unshaven head. "You shouldn't have too much trouble."

"These seem to be for the larger gentleman," Jackson passed Edward a bag. "And these seem to be for the lithe kind of lady," he gave Alley Cat her bag.

He crunched on some sliced wedges of apple as he rifled through his own bag and found some briefs to step into.

"You know the day is truly starting when Jackson chooses to get dressed," Charlotte grimaced. "It's just not usually so early."

"Or so fast," Edward added, grabbing his coffee and a piece of orange while watching Jackson now belt up his new trousers. "Usually Jackson makes dressing and undressing into an art form."

"Usually one does not have a day of engaging with the enemy in mind," Jackson shrugged on his shirt and began buttoning it up.

Alley Cat stretched and fished around in her own bag to begin dressing in the sports-styled attire that had been perfectly selected for her too.

"Alright," Edward gave in. "I suppose I'm just apprehensive about how the day will pan out."

"Just think of Jocelyn," Jackson answered. He came across to help Edward into a shirt, but put a hand on Edward's heart. "The risks will be worth it."

"Where are you going to arrange to meet up with them?" Charlotte asked. "There's free Wi-Fi in the cafés near here. You could do it on neutral grounds."

"We'll actually make contact from the museum," Alley Cat replied. "It will be the most useful place for us."

"But they'll know where you're based," Charlotte frowned. "That's too dangerous."

"Trust me," Alley Cat told her. "It is as necessary as a supportive bra."

When it came time to hug Charlotte goodbye, Jackson pressed her to himself especially firmly, and even turned to shake hands with Mick. Then he wordlessly took Alley Cat around the waist and shadowed her back to the National Museum, with Edward re-materialising beside them in his turn.

"Alright, I'm all set with the things you wanted," The Curator said instead of greeting them. "I have the tracker, the remote control for gallery security, and the doctored cave painting image is loaded onto your scanner with the other pictures. I also cleared the Babylonian tablet corner and got the new paint as you asked."

"How did you go with doctoring the image?" Alley Cat questioned curiously, crossing to join The Curator at his set up of computers. She pocketed the scanner when he handed it to her and gazed at the picture on his screen critically.

"A friend of mine in Paris is a great imitation artist," The Curator explained. "I asked for something that looked like it was part of the collection, but portraying the extra scene that we devised."

"I'm not going to remember if what we pull off today is successful," Alley Cat said. "And I suppose once I'm in I won't really care. But if today's trials play out as hoped, me getting that image to them will be crucial. You won't breach CARE without it."

"If today's experiments don't work," Edward added, "both you and Tiger will not be able to be cured."

"That too," Alley Cat agreed.

The Curator nodded, and turned to beckon Jackson closer. "On that note, I need to inject the tracker."

Jackson grimaced, but extended his forearm to The Curator. "I've spent my whole life avoiding leaving traces, being pinned down or being followed. Now here I am enabling exactly that."

The Curator took little heed of Jackson's reservations, shooting the tracking chip into Jackson's skin. The Curator also took no heed of Jackson's glare.

Alley Cat sat down at The Curator's keyboard and began opening complicated looking windows on the main monitor.

"Never fear," Alley Cat told him. Her windows were full of complex coding now. "If all of our 'ifs' pan out, we'll be able to disable it. If all of our 'ifs' don't pan out, it'll hardly matter."

"No fear here at all," Jackson grumbled, flexing his hand and rolling his sleeve back down to re-button it.

"I'm in," Alley Cat declared. "Sending an invite directly to Mister Marcus Knight's personal CARE account."

"You are an incredible hacker," The Curator shook his head. "No wonder they want you back."

She typed a quick message: 'Tiger's healing and Jocelyn's return can be exchanged for my services. I'll take on your job offer, and give you everything I've analysed about the cave drawings – Alexis Steel.'

She attached a file, which was a map of the museum. There was a circle around the top floor private gallery and office that they currently stood in. Then she pressed send.

"Right," she turned to Jackson. "Darken my memory of the final image being a fake, and of you having a tracker. Then darken my memory of the name and location of Charlotte's Bar."

Jackson reached out and put his hands on her hips, pulling her closer. He let his gaze burn into hers. "But I won't let you forget what happened at Charlotte's bar," he promised. "On any of your visits there." The energy rolled on his voice and rippled the air around them slightly. "You simply need to remember that you want to work for CARE."

Her expression was intent, her eyes not flickering as the shadows passed from him and into her mind, settling thickly over her memories.

"In exchange for help with Tiger and Jocelyn, you have an important image to show CARE," Jackson went on smoothly, but unhappily. "And that image will mean that they will want to bring me in."

"What am I still doing here then?" Alley Cat asked him with a frown.

Jackson sighed. "You were giving me a goodbye kiss before they arrive," he informed her, and drew her right in against him for a heated moment of lips and tongues that made The Curator roll his eyes.

"Ok," Alley Cat, managed after a moment. "All will be fine. Are we ready?"

Jackson pulled her in for one more heated kiss before letting go. "You taste like cinnamon and strawberries," he whispered. "You're lying about it all being fine."

"A lie with the best intentions," she answered with a small smile. Then she stepped away to watch the security monitors.

"Marcus won't be far off," Edward stated. "He knew roughly where in the world I was already, and has likely just been waiting for a sign as to which specific location to hone in on."

"You're right," Alley Cat commented with raised eyebrows, not taking her gaze from the security monitors. The cameras showed footage of Edward's lookalike already standing on the epic front entrance steps to the museum. As Marcus Knight turned to observe the building, two more figures appeared beside him. After a few brief words, they each headed in different directions around the property, and disappeared.

"Three lightlings," Jackson whistled between his teeth. "No zombie humans. Must have been too hard to transport quickly."

"That was Charlotte's twin," Edward observed. "And Xander's twin too. I haven't seen him since Bosnia."

"You still haven't," Alley Cat told him, her eyes flitting from the entrances of the landing above them, to the entrances of the room they stood in. "Remember, Marilyn Peace. And the other one was Jonathon Right."

"My, my!" Marcus Knight's voice declared. Like an apparition, he became suddenly visible across from them. "What a handsome man, Mister Edward Scott. I never had the opportunity to meet you when you visited CARE's headquarters. Seeing any of us would have been quite alarming for you."

"I'm still rather alarmed to see you here," Edward glowered. "Without Jocelyn accompanying you for exchange."

"Anika Sweet is with dear Jocelyn Truth," Charlotte's voice answered – Marilyn Peace appeared on the landing above, leaning on the polished balcony rail. "Anika simply won't part with her opposite."

"Then we won't part with Alley Cat or her scanner," Jackson growled. "You've wasted your time in coming. You should've stayed buried in your cave."

"No," Alley Cat cut in sharply – though she was frowning slightly as she said it. "I want to work with CARE. They can still heal Tiger, and I'll give them the scanner image at the very least."

"Heal Tiger?" there was a laugh as Jonathon Right appeared in a far corner of the lower level. "We have no idea how and no wish to turn our drained lackeys back to ordinary. We've only just started this particular experiment."

"So as I said," Jackson simmered. "You've wasted your time."

"Have we?" Marcus mused. And then in a flash he had disappeared and reappeared in a rush in front of Alley Cat. He splayed one palm across her sternum and wrapped another arm around her shoulders. At once the light played about them as if a filtered ray of sunshine was dancing free of Alley Cat and pouring into Marcus. She sank back against his arm, her wide eyes not just filling with black – but emptying of colour and soul.

"Let's see if she can handle being left with one percent goodness. She'll be the first," Marcus smiled, and then took his hand from her chest to stroke her face. "Where are you going Alexis?" he asked.

"Well," Alley Cat replied in a breathy voice, struggling to stand up without his support. "I'll be going with you."

"Right you are my dear," Marcus congratulated her, before throwing her over his shoulder.

Jackson yelled out in fury, and launched himself at Marcus, but before he collided with the lightling, Marcus threw Alley Cat upward and suddenly Jonathon was sweeping past – half in solid form and half in a kind of light mist. Jonathon caught her mid-air, they both turned to white mist and were gone.

Marilyn laughed a coarse laugh and plunged down from her balcony to land on Jackson's other side. She darted toward him at the same time that Marcus ploughed forward, and Jackson was winded between them until Edward ripped Marilyn backward by her hair so that she yelped and fell.

Edward stomped down on her throat to pin her and the impact brought an explosion of blood and wheezing from the woman.

"Marilyn," Marcus called. "Go home."

Coughing, she disappeared from under Edward's foot at once.

Both Edward and Jackson rounded on Marcus, who started to fade himself. But with a snarl of rage Jackson plunged his hand into the forming mists and took hold of Marcus' head. Or, more specifically, clamped his fist around Marcus' brain so that the lightling couldn't think, let alone turn to nothing.

Jackson threw a burst of darkness into the tightly gripped organ, and Marcus howled in befuddlement, becoming solid once again as he tried desperately to back pedal and to claw at his head.

"Ready?" Jackson shouted, his hand buried in the now visible skull of his opponent.

"Ready," both The Curator and Edward chorused.

Jackson launched both himself and Marcus across the room like two missiles twisting together.

Marcus screamed in pain as he was dragged across the large room by his brain, to be slammed into a corner that had been recently cleared of Babylonian tablets.

At the same time that Jackson turned his hand to shadow, pumping another blast of darkness into Marcus's skull for good measure, Edward yanked Jackson backward and The Curator keyed a command into his remote control.

At once a see-through disaster proof seal hissed down into place over where the Babylonian tablets were usually stored for protection. Before he could recover, Marcus was trapped in the corner, and Jackson was sitting up safely in Edward's arms.

"We don't have much time," The Curator wheeled himself

over quickly. "They'll start asking why he never made it back before the end of the day."

"He'll suffocate before then," Jackson added coolly. "No trying to turn to mist and rainbows to escape," he raised his voice and knocked smugly on the sealed prison. "Air tight. No fissures or pores or little holes."

"The darkness," Marcus cried out with a crazed look in return. "That was amazing."

"Darkness can be addictive," Edward crossed his arms.

"And seductive," Jackson agreed.

"I need another hit!"

"Oh you'll get another hit," Jackson scowled, raising a fist.

"Your hand," The Curator frowned.

Jackson's hand was covered in burns and blisters, and he lowered it regretfully. "Unfortunately I don't seem to have such a joyous reaction to contact with a lightling's essence."

"So our darkness is like a happy drug to lightlings – fun for them to consume. But their light burns and pains us," Edward stated glumly. "That's quite the disadvantage."

"Makes sense," Jackson shrugged.

"I … I can't breathe," Marcus announced, starting to sober up.

"Depressurising environment," The Curator replied. "You'll die soon."

"And if we just paint this sealed panel to hide you, you'll keep dying," Jackson informed the lightling pleasantly. "Every time you rejuvenate, you'll quietly suffocate all over again. No lightling buddies will ever find you when we leave."

"Unless …" Edward drew the word out.

"Unless?" Marcus gasped.

"Unless you do some experiments with us," Jackson answered sinisterly. "I'm guessing they'll be the kind of experiments you've done on Jocelyn, but with you as the guinea pig this time."

Marcus' cheeks were crimson as if they had been pinched, and he was heaving for breaths.

"This is not a nice way to go," The Curator grimaced.

"Especially not a nice way to keep going indefinitely," Edward nodded blandly, examining his fingernails.

"It won't be ... forever," Marcus spat rebelliously. He swallowed with an effort, growing faint. "Paint eventually cracks and someone will see me one day."

"Eventually," Jackson agreed. "One day. That'll be long enough for you to be insane." He turned his back on Marcus. "Let's test it," he suggested calmly. "Show Mister Knight what it's like to come back to life with zero oxygen."

The Curator leaned back in his chair and steepled his fingers. Jackson and Edward dragged their own chairs over to sit and watch.

Marcus tried to glare at them, but there was wild panic in his now bloodshot, bulging eyes.

They sat staring impassively back – unmoved spectators.

The wheezing was increasing, blood vessels were popping in Marcus' eyes and he had slumped right down in his small corner.

"This is the cleanest I've ever been on a torture job," Jackson mused quietly to Edward, who nodded. But they were both intent on Marcus' eyes, which were slowly losing focus – and slowly losing life.

"I'll go fetch Tiger," The Curator announced as those eyes

became vacant and glassy. "Give this guy time to really be dead."

"Do you need help?" Edward asked uncertainly, but The Curator was already wheeling his way over to some seemingly innocent bookshelves, and sliding one forward and to the side like a well-oiled door. A secret passage was revealed within the wall, and The Curator rolled forward confidently.

"I'll use one of Alley Cat's tranquilisers," he called back over his shoulder. "Otherwise, he can't affect me in the same way he affects you."

"He does also have the upper body build of Goliath," Jackson shrugged as The Curator left their view. "He'll be fine." He rose to prowl toward the barrier between them and Marcus. "This one on the other hand," he said speculatively, "might stay dead longer than we want."

"What do you suggest?" Edward asked.

"Well we did only recently break his heart and drop a cave on him, so he's surely in bad shape," Jackson reflected. "What if you lift the seal a crack and I try shooting some of the good stuff at him again? Shock him awake on good, ol energising badness?"

Edward's eyes flickered to where The Curator had left the controller, and then back to Marcus, uncertain.

"Come on," Jackson coaxed. "Just a sliver. If it works, he gets a hit, we close it up again and teach him another lesson. If it doesn't work, we close it up again, wait for an annoying and risky amount of time and then teach him another lesson. Rinse and repeat."

Edward took a breath and reached for the controller. Its screen was still on and ready, and with a fast jab Edward hit the 'lift' button so that the seal hissed upward. With a grin, Jackson sent a jet of darkness into the small space that hit Marcus' body with an effect like an electric shock – dead limbs flailing and jerking. Then Edward hit the 'close' option and the seal hissed down again.

"Worth it," Jackson smirked quietly. "Worked like a defibrillator."

And Edward saw Marcus sitting bolt upright, boggling, as he was already starting to suffocate again. He didn't even have enough air to cry out or to lift his hand to clutch his throat.

"Can you imagine how many times you would have to wake up and die like this before anyone might come near an ordinary painted wall?" Jackson went on for Marcus' benefit. "I wonder how long you could actually go at it, before your essence just starved and snuffed out."

The Curator wheeled himself back in, with Tiger slumped limply across his legs. He closed the passage and brought Tiger to the base of the sealed prison, where he laid Tiger down.

"Our major curiosity," Jackson told Marcus, "is whether or not you can fix what you have done to Alley Cat and Tiger. It would have been easier if you'd just helped us with this when you first arrived, but are you willing to have a go at it now?"

Marcus nodded frantically.

"Good," Jackson crooned. "We'll just let you have this next death and then we'll begin."

Marcus' brow knitted in despair, but Jackson ignored this as the lightling dwindled back to an empty corpse again.

"So, conundrum," Jackson said to The Curator and Edward. "We want Marcus to be too weak to escape, but we want Marcus strong enough to try fixing Tiger. Suggestions?"

"Like you did before, you could try gripping some other important organ to keep him in check," The Curator offered.

"Ew," Jackson frowned. "I'm not touching his other important organ."

"Not quite so low," The Curator rolled his eyes.

"His heart," Edward agreed. "Then if he causes trouble or you want to neutralise and trap him again, you just give the heart a squeeze and stop it."

"Alright," Jackson rubbed his chin. "Could work. But keep the controller on hand."

Jackson reached forward and grabbed The Curator's belt – unbuckling it rapidly while The Curator gaped in surprise.

"What?" Jackson grinned. "It's not like you need it. They're not going to fall down." He swatted away The Curator's hand and whipped the belt free, ducking under the lifting barrier when Edward pressed the 'lift' button on the controller again.

"You're enjoying this," The Curator accused as Jackson began strapping Marcus' wrists together.

"We could all be dead by tomorrow," Jackson replied cheerfully. "Why dwell?"

Then he turned one of his hands to shadow, and plunged it into Marcus' chest, along with another shot of darkness.

There was a horrific, dry rasping as Marcus went rigid and opened his eyes wide and gurgling.

"Oops, dear me," Jackson announced cajolingly. "That was a lung. How embarrassing." He thrust forward harder. "Ahh, even after Alley Cat's efforts, you do have one. Or I have it," he amended. "Your heart, that is. So no funny business."

Marcus was gaping like a fish, but managed to nod.

The Curator reached down and put Tiger's wrist into the bound hands of the lightling. "Try putting the light back into this young man," he instructed.

Marcus blinked – suddenly unwilling.

Jackson tutted, and gave a tug with his fingers so that Marcus cried out. But he closed his eyes in concentration and Jackson could feel that something was happening within the lightling.

Tiger jerked a little.

"No man!" Tiger whimpered even in his sleep. "No, take it back."

The Curator lifted one of Tiger's eyelids. "The colour is less stark," he observed. "But not normal."

"Keep going Mister Knight," Jackson purred, but beads of sweat had started to roll down Marcus' face, and the skin had started to seem tight against Marcus' skull.

"Huh," Edward grunted with raised eyebrows.

Marcus' nose had started to drizzle blood that ran down his now sallow cheek.

"Please take it back. I like how I am," Tiger sobbed.

"Ahhh," Jackson blinked up at The Curator and Edward. "So Marcus just died again. Without my help."

"You did say he was in bad shape," Edward said, but with an expression of consternation.

"And the cave paintings did show that giving the light was taxing on lightlings," The Curator added.

"I guess that level of effort would be enough to make the good guys go bad," Jackson mused. Then he pumped Marcus' heart with his fist and shot another burst of darkness into him.

Marcus was snivelling when he was jolted back to life this time.

"Come on," Jackson encouraged, with a smile like a wolf's. "Tiger isn't back to his normal self yet. Keep going."

Jackson kept reviving Marcus until the lightling clearly had nothing left, and after a final push of light Tiger was sleeping peacefully. Then Jackson hauled Marcus' alive but lolling body back, squashing it into the small corner space again.

"Sorry," Jackson told the helplessly gaping Marcus. "I lied. This corner still needs a lick of paint. And we could possibly still need a captive lightling."

The seal closed once more, and Marcus stared in limp horror, already suffocating as Jackson and Edward quickly worked rollers up and down the entire length of his chamber.

"I hope that's fast drying," The Curator said. "Because we have company. Again."

| 22 |

Regroup

"There are more of them this time," The Curator said urgently, before he keyed in a new code that switched off the power to the office.

All the lights and screens immediately darkened and there was the loud hissing of every other seal automatically sliding down to protect the artefacts against the walls.

"Of course," Jackson hid the paint and rollers. "We have their Vice President. I'm kind of curious to hang around and see all our friends in doppelganger form."

"Stifle that curiosity," Edward told him dryly, hefting Tiger over his shoulder.

They retreated after The Curator as he led the way into the secret passage once more, and closed the bookshelf styled door behind them.

"This way," The Curator instructed, wheeling quickly down the dim corridor as they followed.

"We'll exit somewhere they'll least expect in case they've left any lightlings to watch for us."

He was able to move much faster than Edward and Jackson on foot, so they ghosted after him in shadow form until he silently gestured to a trapdoor-like hatch in the wall.

Jackson materialised properly and stooped to pull the hatch open, a quizzical frown on his brow as he peered down at what seemed to be a dark slide.

The Curator levered himself out of his chair and into the hatch. He gave them a salute and then pushed off, disappearing immediately.

They waited long enough for The Curator to have slid down a few floors before Edward lowered Tiger's unconscious form onto the slide entrance.

"Down the hatch," Jackson mouthed, and Edward launched Tiger off. Then the darklings turned to shadow and whipped their way down the slide too.

"Got you," they heard The Curator say as he caught Tiger, and they slowed as they exited the slide to find themselves in a new passage with flickering white emergency lights.

"I'm lost," Jackson admitted, pulling Tiger up and over his shoulder while The Curator angled himself into a new chair that had obviously been left there for such times.

"We're out of the walls and now we're underground," The Curator explained, already wheeling forward again. "We just slid down an industrial chute in the museum wall, but now we're moving under the carpark to the perimeter of the property."

"Clever," Edward complimented the man, hurrying after him.

"You're being trusted with a great deal of knowledge on this place," The Curator replied. "Quite the honour."

He leaned forward, the veins in his forearms standing out as he pushed his way up a now climbing slope.

"Move quickly," he instructed when they reached a dead end to the tunnel, with a round man-hole cover in the ceiling being the only exit. There were loops of metal protruding from the wall, leading up to the man-hole like a ladder.

The Curator strapped and buckled his legs to the chair like an athlete, and used the metal loops to pull his own body weight and that of his chair upwards. With a grunt, he forced the man-hole cover aside so that the evening's light filtered down over them.

"We could have helped," Jackson muttered while The Curator somehow drew himself up and out to the surface.

"Obviously unneeded," Edward chuckled, launching himself up and out too.

"Well, I suppose we'll follow suit," Jackson told Tiger, lifting off from the tunnel floor and landing outside on a strip of grass. They were near a long hedge that bordered the expansive museum lands, and they would have been near impossible to notice by any watching eyes focused on the distant museum itself.

"This van is our ticket out," The Curator announced, wheeling across to a sleek vehicle and unlocking the rear door for them.

At once an automatic ramp lowered from the back of the car so that The Curator could enter, rolling himself right to the front of the vehicle.

"Wow," Edward commented. "Those are some great modifications."

There were military style bench seats on either side of the

back of the van, with hand holds dangling from the ceiling. There were no other seats in the front, instead The Curator's chair was locked into place by clamps that closed around the wheels as he reached them.

He pressed a button for the ignition and took hold of the steering wheel before peering back over his shoulder at them, eyebrows raised. His fingers were poised over a speed dial to get them going.

"Right you are," Jackson agreed. He laid Tiger out on the open space between the bench seats and then he and Edward jumped in, closing the doors behind them and grabbing their hand holds.

Within minutes the van was pulling out smoothly to join the flow of traffic as sight-seers and researchers left the museum for the day.

"Oh man!" Tiger uttered when they had left the museum far behind to drive through the inner city. He opened his eyes and squinted up at Jackson. "I need some filling in!" he demanded tiredly, though with his usual good natured tone.

"You've got time," The Curator told them, weaving across lanes and passing glittering high rises.

"Boss man!" Tiger cried out, leaning up on his elbows. "Actually … I think I know a fair bit already. I just don't believe it."

"Believe it," Edward replied, and explained a succinct version of events to the young, newly restored explorer.

"So you're proof that Alley Cat and the other drained people can be helped," Jackson finished for Edward. "But we haven't got to the bottom of how to deal with the lightlings as an overall issue."

"And right now we are stalling our next contact to make sure they've had time to view Alley Cat's false image," The Curator added.

"Well," Tiger rubbed his face blearily, dragging himself up onto a bench seat. "At the very least it sounds like you put a stop to Marcus Knight."

"Temporarily," Jackson waved his still blistered hand dismissively. "And there's no point even trying to find a way of killing them permanently, because more would appear to balance things out."

"Probably the only reason we're not dead yet too, seeing as they actually do have a way to kill us off," Edward grimaced.

"At least maybe you could reason with new lightlings?" Tiger offered helpfully.

"You're too optimistic," Jackson told him. "Eventually new lightlings would become as bitter and burnt out as these ones have. And they would become just as self-serving for their own survival. I know I would."

"But they're supposed to be wired to be good. And we could control them," Edward mused. "We could oversee things. We would know about them this time."

"Nah," Tiger sat forward. "Things aren't natural at the moment. The balance needs to be properly restored."

"I don't suppose the lightlings have had all these same thoughts," The Curator commented. He was now pulling into an underground carpark to a particularly glamourous high rise.

"But perhaps they decided they would be the ones doing the controlling."

"Well," Jackson slumped. "It sure doesn't pay to be behind

the eight ball. I can't believe the darklings have lost in the race to create devious plans."

"But, unlike lightlings," Tiger countered, crossing his arms. "Darklings shouldn't take the easy, devious way out. They should find a real solution to fix things."

"Why do the good guys get to have all the fun?" Jackson sighed. But he was re-energised and duly impressed when he was shown around the high tech penthouse that The Curator had brought them to.

"Like the museum," The Curator explained, "this place has managed to remain independent. It is run by The Proprietor, an old college mate of mine with similar views. We're safe in any of his establishments." He switched on a series of monitors at a desk that backed onto epic views of the city skyline. "I chose this one because Alley Cat has never visited it."

"It's great," Jackson replied. "Now everyone leave me alone. I'm off to find a hot shower and a posh bed. Phase two begins tomorrow." He was already loosening his collar. "And as a key player, I need my beauty sleep."

| 23 |

Contact

It was early, with dawn just breaking. But they had only just caught her before she'd left.

He heard the roar of her motorbike starting up. The satisfying tester rev as she settled in to ride.

The roller door to her apartment building was sliding upward as the headlight of the bike appeared and she sped forward – bursting out onto the road and tearing toward him.

Jackson stoically held his ground in the middle of the road, and she skidded to a stop with barely a meter between them.

"Alley Cat," The Curator rolled out onto the asphalt from one side while Tiger and Edward stepped out on the other side, cutting off the road ahead of her. "We have cured Tiger. We can help you too."

She cocked her head to the side before she slowly removed her helmet. She blinked cold, black eyes at him.

"You presume that I want a 'cure'," she said. "And you presume that I won't just drive right through you."

"We presumed that you would be drawn back to your

apartment," Jackson countered. "And we were right about that."

Alley Cat eyed him with faint amusement. And with a touch of desire.

"But did you guess that I would bring friends?" she asked. "Or that I would be willing to share my treasured things with them?"

There was the sound of many bikes revving to life then. And a row of single headlights cruised into view as a line of others like Alley Cat rode out to circle them.

"But let's not bicker," she told Jackson. "Mister White specifically wishes to meet you."

Jackson crossed his arms. "Tell him to just look in the mirror."

She cast a glance over Jackson's shoulder and suddenly the other black-eyed people were kicking down their motorbike stands and stepping off.

"Your new friends are a bad influence on you," Jackson admonished.

"I'm the one with the influence," Alley Cat smirked, and with a wave of her hand, the others were now charging forward.

Tiger ducked as a fist was thrown toward his face, and The Curator maneuvered himself through two attackers like a bowling ball ramming pins out of the way. But Edward staggered a little as one of the female assailants jumped lithely up on his back – her forearm squeezed against his throat. His eyes went wide as the darkness rolled off the woman and into him, and he hurriedly moved to throw her off.

"Let's party," Alley Cat announced, getting off her own bike and stalking toward Jackson.

Jackson shivered, almost captivated by her and the energy she exuded, but he blinked when one attacker threw a boot into The Curator's chair so that he was upended and thrown sideways – landing bodily on the pavement.

Jackson dodged Alley Cat's advance and slammed into The Curator's attacker, feeling the enticing sting of the drug-like darkness poisoning the man.

The attacker sprawled on the pavement, and Jackson quickly seized and pinned the man's legs down under his grip.

"Have a ..." Jackson leaned downward and crushed the man's legs against the sidewalk. "Little empathy!" he thrust harder on the man's shins so that the two tibias cracked and sank while the man howled.

Already feeling the heady effects of touching a man drained of too much goodness, Jackson sprang up and righted The Curator's chair. He could tell Edward felt it too as the darkling roared and charged at an opponent.

"He's here," Jackson heard Alley Cat say, and he turned to find her hanging up a call.

But even before he had finished turning, there was a flash of brilliant light in front of him, and he found himself stepping into the arms of his twin.

Mister White's smile was almost tender as he gazed down at Jackson and sank a talon knife into Jackson's stomach. It slid in up to the hilt, and Mister White moved it upward to rest under Jackson's breastbone.

"No!" Edward gasped.

Jackson sank against Mister White, gripping the

lightling's waist in an effort to stay upright. Mister White caught Jackson under the arms as if they were embracing. But Jackson's blood was colouring Mister White's suit crimson.

"Edward," Jackson managed. "Get them out of here."

Looking incredibly pained, Edward threw a dark eyed man off of himself and tore a woman off Tiger. Then Edward grabbed both The Curator and Tiger's wrists, and they all disappeared.

"That's fine," Mister White said, holding Jackson close. "You're what I was after."

"I'm bleeding all over your fancy outfit," Jackson smirked almost drunkenly. His eyelids were weighted.

"Also fine," Mister White smiled benevolently. "Let's get you back to CARE and cleaned up."

"We'll meet you," Alley Cat said, getting ready to mount her bike again.

"Not all of you," Mister White negated. "Jerome is useless now."

"Of course," Alley Cat agreed, crossing to the man with the broken legs. She knelt beside him and gripped his head. Then she deftly smashed the back of his skull against the concrete, repetitively, until he'd reached a messy oblivion.

"Well done," Mister White crooned. Before light surrounded him, burning and turning Jackson to mist – and sapping the last of the life from him.

| 24 |

Awakening

"He's reviving."

The room was dim with red lighting.

A heavy, gluggy blink did not make it easier for Jackson to see, but he could make out faint movements in the corner of the room.

"Why were you after Jackson Flint, specifically?" a purring voice asked from the corner.

Alley Cat's voice. Jackson strained his eyes, and as if she were a mirage emerging from red mists, Jackson began to make her out. Alley Cat was swinging gently on a hoop that was suspended from the high ceiling. Like an acrobat – or pet canary.

Her lips had been painted black to match her eyes, and she now wore a skin tight black cat suit that clung to her body like water under a midnight sky. The neckline plunged all the way down to below her sternum – a sharp arrow pointing to her naval. Breathtaking.

"And why me?" she asked. "After all the allies I took from you."

"You are extraordinary," Mister White's voice replied, and Jackson only then realised that the lightling was standing close, watching him. "And he is necessary. Important. Your images proved that."

Jackson's back was pressed against a regal bedhead, his arms stretched out and his wrists bound tightly to its posts. He winced as Mister White leaned across the bed to cup his jawline, angling Jackson's face to observe their likeness more closely.

Alley Cat's eyes glittered as if she had been possessed, but her expression suggested that she was merely faintly curious as she turned her gaze to Jackson.

"Now it is clearer than ever that our other halves are key to our success or failure," Mister White went on. His touch on Jackson's jaw was stinging, as if Jackson's skin was being singed. "So my other half is especially important above all."

"You want to make yourself whole again? Reunite the halves like the last picture showed?" Alley Cat asked.

Mister White's grip tightened on Jackson's face for a moment, and a flash of heat scorched Jackson's skin before the lightling simply released his hold. Mister White straightened and crossed to Alley Cat.

"Quite the opposite. That would be to lose myself," Mister White explained patiently. He ran his fingers slowly down the centre of her plunging neckline. "That last picture was the exact reason I wanted to get my hands on Mister Flint – to avoid our joining, and to give me the chance to take control of him instead." He didn't take his touch away from her skin for many long moments. "We have learned from our experiments with Miss Jocelyn that it is too likely that a darkling would consume us and snuff us out." He circled around her to take hold of the hoop, pulling it back. "That is what they do. We give, and they take."

"Or that's how it was meant to be," Jackson managed to croak.

"Yes," Mister White agreed pleasantly. He released the hoop so that Alley Cat swung gently out and away from him, before he caught her again. "We were on the back foot from our very beginnings, as my very early paintings show. And if we hadn't been, the world would be a different place. The place that CARE now hopes to create, after all of this time."

"You ..." Jackson fought to sit more comfortably. "You didn't even remember what you painted. You had to find the cave again to work out what you were upset about."

"A perfect example of our disadvantage," Mister White sighed. He twirled the hoop around so that Alley Cat faced him, and he kept hold of the hoop – gripping either side with his hands over hers. "From the start darklings were able to do their part. Darkness can be impulsive, or calculated – both traits that mean a darkling learns fast and becomes clever. On the other hand, goodness has to develop. It starts slow as simple innocence and trust. It can build up to heroics and pure intentions, but it is always slow and strengthens only when challenged – if it is not destroyed in the process. Which means we were naïve, oblivious for too long, and our challenges were too harsh. I started mindlessly, while my counterpart began to strengthen immediately."

"Which is fortunate," Jackson spat. "Isn't it? Considering

you weren't doing your bit. If we hadn't been around to suck the darkness out of people, it would have overwhelmed the world."

Mister White released Alley Cat's hands so that the hoop rotated back around, but she shifted gracefully to sit on the side, one leg perched up on the hoop so that she could still see the lightling.

"Darklings revel in corruption and wrongness. You feed on it, but don't end it," Mister White spoke to Jackson, but softly smoothed and tucked Alley Cat's hair behind her ear. "Lightlings seek order. Goodness and light are clean, organised, peaceful, and without chaos. Yet that is hard to come by."

Jackson snorted. "Of course it is, if you're busy eating up all the goodness that does exist. You're not holding up your end of the bargain, and you're definitely not setting people up to be at their best – peaceful and ordered and blah, blah, blah."

"Quite so," Mister White agreed. "At the start we did try to flood select individuals with goodness to be heroes and models to the rest. But they were too few and far between. We couldn't spread enough goodness, and even though your kind could absorb all the darkness – people were becoming numb rather than better and the world was just getting messier and colder."

"Still is," Alley Cat agreed with a delicate shrug. "People are blank."

"They are, darling one," Mister White agreed. "They are blank, the world is broken … and we lightlings are hungry for better."

"Get a burger," Jackson rolled his eyes.

"The world is trapped by extremes and cycles," Mister White went on. "One persecuted group overthrows their persecutors and then takes their place. Some die of starvation, others of obesity. Some places burn, others flood. The world needs order," he said calmly. "The world needs us to give it that order."

"How can such a large task be accomplished?" Alley Cat questioned.

"We're nearly there," Mister White smiled in a paternal way. "CARE controls all technology, business and travel. We have been carefully stirring up enmity and distrust across the globe so that each nation remains separate and less unified than ever. When we flick the switch on their tech, and close up their borders, they will be too weak to oppose us. We will have complete control over the many peoples of this world. We will force them to be better, without needing to give them the light from our own selves. No more war, no more environmental destruction. Just an orderly, stress-free, pastoral life that people will be grateful for. Where goodness can grow, and lightlings can consume as freely and as without risk as darklings always have."

"Where you can brainwash people into being your smorgasbord," Jackson countered. "Basically you're saying that you're going to groom people into becoming the creatures you want them to be, and then you'll farm humanity. Keep them separate and divided, each country like a pasture of specialised, goodness enriched meat. But I have news for you –" Jackson grimaced. "It doesn't matter how separate you keep the countries. If they can't turn on enemies in other places, they'll find enemies within. Darkness stirs up in small groups and in solitary beings as much as it does across oceans."

"An unfortunate truth," Mister White nodded. "And the reason that I have a very special place in my plan for the darklings."

Jackson laughed. "Lightlings like order. Darklings like freedom. I don't think you'll find us to be very helpful."

"Hence why we have needed to make our little experiments and refinements on Miss Truth," Mister White smiled too. "And why I have specially wanted the most influential of all darklings to be next in line for our conditioning process."

Jackson felt his blood chill. "I don't take it you mean I'm going to have silky hair after this."

Mister White finally stepped away from Alley Cat, straightening his white tie and crossing to the bedroom, or holding bay, door. "Your conditioning will be much more profound than a salon treatment. We'll be making you into the very thing that will help us to control any imbalances of darkness in our 'farms' while we try to boost up the goodness. You won't take me over, but you will join with me – and follow me."

Mister White opened the door to admit three women, and Jackson's stomach tightened.

Charlotte's twin, Marilyn Peace. Jocelyn's twin, Anika Sweet. And Jocelyn herself.

"Darklings must be controlled," Jocelyn announced. "We must be used to create control."

"Yes, dear," Mister White kissed her hand. "You understand that now."

"Hello Jocelyn," Jackson managed. He couldn't keep the

dismay from his face. It was very clear that she had lost herself.

"Jackson, when I first came to you it was because of the overwhelming darkness that was growing among the uneducated, brutish tribes of the Dark Ages," Jocelyn replied. "That was because the lightlings had first experimented in taking the light they needed during the fall of Rome. But they realised that that level of drainage was not sustainable," she said earnestly. "They waited for this long, hungering and desperate, to make sure that they were ready and in control, and could get things right."

"And to get things right," Marilyn added, "we need the very best darkling sheep dogs working for us to keep the herds in check."

"With darklings under our guidance, we will become the guardian angels of humanity. The leaders," Anika finished.

"The conquerors ..." Jackson muttered. "You'll be so dark by then yourselves that your 'sheep dogs' will be able to feed off you."

"Funny," Marilyn told him. "But you'll be too well trained to turn on your masters."

"They perfected the training on me," Jocelyn explained. "But with you on our side, all the others will fall into line."

"Well, I suppose the process has started," Jackson drawled. "Because this has been torture enough."

Mister White moved out of the way to watch, leaning against an ornate mantelpiece over an unlit fire. There was a jug full of iced water on the mantel, and Jackson ached for it.

But he watched with narrowed eyes as Anika and Marilyn

came to sit on either side of Jackson, while Jocelyn sat at Jackson's feet.

"Think of Jocelyn as your personal defibrillator," Anika told Jackson sweetly as she unbuttoned his shirt.

"I died so often during the conditioning process that it really wasted time," Jocelyn explained. "I'll speed up your recovery so we can get this done faster."

"Thanks," Jackson muttered.

"I'll also drain you of your darkness," Jocelyn added conversationally.

"My …?" Jackson strained to sit up straighter.

"Your essence," Jocelyn nodded.

Jackson gapes. Quiet and stumped. No darkling had ever drained another darkling. It was like cannibalism.

"We need to change who you are and how you think before we give your powers back to you," Anika told him clinically.

"We'll start with short bursts of light into your core," Marilyn said, tracing her fingertips across the smooth skin of his stomach and leaving a searing crimson line.

Jackson gasped and then fought to grit his teeth. He could feel the light she had sent into him flickering beneath the surface and through the layers of his flesh like an ember growing and burning through plaster and then wood. Every flicker was gutting agony.

"It'll build up your stamina and tolerance," Marilyn went on, scratching her way over his left nipple. "But the end goal is to fill you up with light and erase your current self completely. Then we can re-make you as we want before you get some of your darkness back."

Anika pulled his shirt open further and pressed her hand to the pulse point in his neck. The light she sent into him was like an electric shock and he cried out despite himself.

"Can I have him when he's fixed?" Alley Cat asked, her tone both curious and removed. "We can be partners."

"You will be too enticing for him to feed on in your current state," Mister White said over the sound of a new, louder groan from Jackson. "But you will have me."

Jackson glowered, panting as he watched Mister White return to where Alley Cat lounged. And the lightling pulled her hoop close to him and kissed her – long and slow.

"You taste like candy apples," Alley Cat said at last.

Jackson cried out again.

"You taste like sugar and cream," Mister White replied. "Naughty and nice. But ninety-nine percent naughty."

"Alright Jocelyn," Marilyn said. "Take a little darkness, make some room, and let's see how he handles some extra light."

Jackson was breathing heavily, and squeezed his eyes shut with dread as Jocelyn placed her hand on his ankle.

Jackson hunched in on himself and moaned sickly as Jocelyn started to drain his darkness. It felt like someone was tugging at Jackson's insides, trying to pluck something essential, like his organs free of his body.

"Stop," Anika said then. "There's enough room for more light now."

"You are almost too sweet," Alley Cat frowned at Mister White, speaking over Jackson's cries.

But Mister White turned back to the bed as he saw a building glow of white light. The light was increasing beneath Marilyn's fingers as she splayed them over Jackson's chest. It was as if she held a torch against her palm and the light was showing through her pink skin.

"Oh that might have been too far," Anika stated. "He's dying."

"Give him a very small shot of darkness to keep him with us," Marilyn instructed Jocelyn. "Until he's ready for us to rip everything out without being completely destroyed."

"Yes, that's good," Anika said. "His eyes have stopped rolling back."

"Is he already up to this level of dosing?" Mister White enquired with interest. "It won't make him useless?"

"Jocelyn is keeping him on track," Marilyn replied. "We'll get this first drowning and draining done and then rest him."

"Sickly sweet," Alley Cat said quietly, touching her lips where Mister White had kissed her.

"Again. Take the darkness while we force in the light," Anika told Jocelyn as she added her own glowing hand to where Marilyn's light streamed into Jackson's centre.

Jackson screamed as he felt the invisible energies that made up who he was catching fire from the light and being wrenched apart inside himself as Jocelyn tore them away. He arched against the bedframe, the tendons in his neck standing out and his wrists chafing against their ropes.

The moment seemed to stretch on and on as they forced a war to rage within his core, and Alley Cat could not help but frown as she watched.

"Alright," Anika stated. "Jocelyn, leave him just enough darkness to live."

"He's full up on light," Marilyn nodded with satisfaction.

The sweat stood out on Jackson's brow and exposed, burnt skin as he sagged and stared in winded shock.

"Next step is to send the light into his brain too," Anika wiped her hands on Jackson's shirt and stood. "Get both the essence and the mind."

Marilyn stood too, crossing to the door. "We need a break," she told Mister White. "As you know, it's much less fun to give light than to take it."

Mister White smiled benevolently at them. "Of course," he acquiesced. "Sweet pea," he addressed Alley Cat then, and he stroked her lower lip with his thumb. "Keep an eye on Mister Flint. But don't get too close to him, or you'll just charge him back up."

Marilyn laughed, and pulled Jocelyn up by her wrist. "Your minion better not undo all our work."

"Alexis is the most skilful guard alive. And now, completely obedient," Mister White smiled again, following them from the room.

| 25 |

Frenzy

"Who knew it would be so interesting here," Alley Cat told her prisoner with a painted black smile. She let the swing rock back and forth playfully. "I'm glad I brought you across."

Jackson was shuddering, his body wracked with waves of pain.

"There's a phoenix rising from the ashes in your eyes you know," Alley Cat remarked. "An orange light that they put there."

"I'd believe it," Jackson cringed and gasped, doubling over as far as his bonds would allow.

"It's a shame that they're going to make you different," Alley Cat mused. "I like you."

"That's my darkness that you're attracted to," Jackson answered painfully, closing his eyes and letting his head hang forward. "They filled you with it, and darkness is alluring."

"But look at you, that can't be it," Alley Cat replied. "They've filled you up with light."

Jackson squinted up at her. "Ahh. Then it's the darkness in

you. Making you defiant. He told you that you can't have me. So that is what you want. Perhaps they went too far in their experiment with you, and made themselves a rebel."

"They made me to want him. To serve him," she commented. "Completely obedient, remember? But he tastes wrong. Over ripe. Sweet on the surface, rotten underneath."

Jackson's skin was prickling with goose-bumps and sweat – feverish.

"He said it himself," Jackson told her. "You're extraordinary. Though he doesn't seem to have really thought through how different and risky that makes you ... He thinks it makes you a prized slave." Jackson took a deep, steadying breath. "But really, you probably retained parts of yourself, and the strongest parts were likely heightened rather than subdued."

"I think you're extraordinary. And, while I shouldn't," she said slowly. Then she slid forward off her swing and took the jug of iced water from the mantel. "I think I'll play with you. Carefully."

Breathing heavily, Jackson watched as she approached his bedside, plucking an ice cube from the chilled water. Wary not to get too close, or to let her skin touch his, she lowered the ice to his lips.

With a groan, he sucked the ice into his mouth, feeling the comfort of the cool while the rest of his body seared hotly inside and out.

"You know," she said, delicately setting a new cube of ice to balance in the dip between his collar bones. Immediately the ice began to melt against his heated skin, and little slivers of water ran down his scorched chest in rivulets. "When he said they had tried to flood a few people with goodness to guide the others, I thought that was foolish." She placed another cube of ice in his naval so that drops trailed down over his stomach and hips. "Because a real hero should still have some darker qualities, like defiance. And they shouldn't be too pure, or how can they really lead and inspire? It's not impressive to be perfect without having to overcome any flaws."

"Not impressive," Jackson moaned. "Not even likeable."

"Downright annoying," she smirked. "And it wouldn't be right to take all of the darkness from someone either. They would have nothing to enjoy."

"No vices, no sins," Jackson agreed. "Just like they're doing to me."

"A crying shame," Alley Cat sympathised. "But I can't help you," she teased, dancing back from the bed and splashing water over him so that he moaned again. "That would be naughty. One hundred percent naughty."

"That would be rebellious," Jackson nodded as she set the jug back on the mantel. "Wild," he added with an effort. "Which is what you should be embracing, based on what they've made you into."

"That does sound better than just obeying," she drew closer again. "And it's not fair that the others get to touch you, when I asked."

"Touch me," Jackson said. "I promise not to take advantage. We'll just have one last intimate moment."

"You're all goodness and light now," Alley Cat grinned, tentatively reaching a hand out to sweep the hair from his brow. "So I can probably trust your promise."

He sucked a breath in, but her black eyes glittered as she

saw that he was true to his word – doing his best to absorb nothing from her.

Then she was quick to join him on the bed, straddling him and holding his shoulders. With wicked glee she ran her tongue over the little pool of water that had been left by the ice between his collarbones. Then she bit at his neck and laughed softly as he moaned with desire.

"You're not meant to feel lustful anymore, are you Mister Flint?" she purred. "That's not a good, wholesome trait."

"They haven't finished conditioning me," he husked and then gasped as her lips trailed to his nipple. "I'm drowning in goodness, but I'm not perfect."

"Beg to differ," she murmured against him while her hand trailed down to undo his belt and zipper.

She forced her fingers down to where his length strained against his boxer briefs, and took hold – putting pressure on the base of his stiffness.

"Wait," Jackson cautioned, breathing heavily. "I won't be able to keep from drinking you in if you take much more of my focus. I'm on fire here."

She ran her hand back up the length of him and used her other hand to slam his shoulders roughly back against the bedhead. "It's always 'wait' with you," she growled. "But here I am, all greedy and gluttonous. I don't think I'll wait any longer."

She forced a fiery kiss against his lips, letting her tongue play against his and pressing herself against him so that he was in an agony of pleasure and pain.

"Alley Cat," he pleaded breathlessly as she moved her grip back down his stiff length. "Not like this."

"Not like what?" she crooned, and suddenly she was ripping his shoes, pants and briefs right down and off.

It was obvious that he wanted her, and she eyed him greedily as she tore at her body suit, stripping herself naked, ready to straddle him again. To take him into herself no matter what he or Mister White said.

He nodded at his wrists. "Not like this."

She paused.

"Remember, what we agreed?" Jackson said. "When it's time for you and I to connect, it will be about you and I. Nobody and nothing else. I want to give you everything I have to give."

Alley Cat considered it. Remembering. Then nodded slowly. "I do want to enjoy this. With you enjoying it too."

She leaned over him, pert breasts within biting distance, and untied first one wrist and then the other so that he could take hold of her. His hands on her bare back, pulling her to sit against himself so that her skin was on his.

"I can feel your heartbeat we're so close," she purred, taking hold of his face and drawing him in to a much more languid and rolling, sensual kiss.

Despite the roiling energies inside him, Jackson held onto her and unhurriedly levered their bodies downward so that she was lying on top of him. He ran one hand down to rest on her lower back while the other cupped her breasts and massaged her nipples, and she reached down to encircle his cock with her fingers again – running her hand up and down as she tried to pull him into place.

Instead of letting her sink down over him, he rolled her onto the mattress beside himself and leaned up, pushing her legs apart as he claimed her lips with fevered kisses again. He cupped her between the legs and teasingly worked his fingers over and then finally into her while her pelvis thrust against him – building her up from a playful state, to one that was overcome with wanting.

Her hold on his throbbing cock became so insistent as she neared the edge of orgasm that at last he let his hips follow her guidance. And she pulled him into place on top of her.

"Give me everything you've got," she urged. "As promised."

Jackson's eyes held hers as he lowered himself until he felt his tip touch her entrance. And then he unhurriedly, deliberately thrust in. First enveloping his tip – then the rest of his shaft as he let it slowly enter her.

It was almost too much for him to bear in his current state. A relief. And she groaned as she took him into herself, feeling the pushing of the fullness of him as they pressed themselves right up against each other.

He gripped one of her hips with one hand and put pressure on her lower back with the other so that he dragged her down against himself again, and he watched the pure pleasure on her face as he made sure to rub the right places and on the right angles.

She let him control the rolling, pressing movements as they melted into each other, and she did not care as he let more and more of what was within himself go each time.

Other than darkening memories, or torturing Marcus Knight, he'd never done this before – given something from inside of himself away to another in a completely intimate way. That was a lightling's job. And he was in such a state of bliss and fever that he was nearly too overcome to do it carefully.

But like spreading shadows to darken people's memories, he could do something similar with his light now if he just tried with all of his will not to lose himself in the moment.

"Do you trust me?" he husked against her ear as she leaned into him in a state of total abandon.

"Do what you want!" she cried out in ecstasy. "Keep going!"

He clasped the back of her neck and kissed her shoulder as he slithered a hand down to her clitoris and touched tingling, warm fingers there – stroking her and letting the dancing energy spread into her so that she almost wailed.

He stroked and pushed in and drew back so that she could feel every single thing. And he ravished every inch of skin he could reach with his mouth until every part of her was electrified and heightened to beyond sensitivity.

The muscles in their abdomens were tensing, their feet were arching, their pelvic muscles were seizing – and he dragged her against himself, thrusting into her as if every pulsing movement was the most important he would ever make.

He forced out the light that Marilyn and Anika had so generously given him. Letting it drum into Alley Cat, pounding into her with each motion, while he let his guard down totally and absorbed the life-saving darkness she could give him.

The intolerable burning left his centre, the cooling darkness flooded in. The shadows fell from her memory, the darkness slipped from her body and the goodness rushed in.

She dragged her fingernails down his back, he arched up into her and held her to himself. He gasped into her shoulder while she clenched and squeezed around him, her legs locking him into place. They gasped and filled each other and pushed together until he gave her the final, dragging, pressing thrusts that sent them both over the edge and gave them both the release they had so desperately wanted.

And when Alley Cat sank into him and held him close, it was with a true smile and clear eyes. The balance restored to her soul.

"Well that was worth the wait," she murmured, and kissed his neck. "You tasted like honey."

| 26 |

Revelations

"Alexis, Mister White has requested you –" Anika's sentence ended in a gasp as she opened the door to the scene of Jackson and Alley Cat's heated tryst. "You – you ...!" Anika sputtered furiously.

"What is it?" Jocelyn's voice came from the hall. She stepped in and regarded them with surprise.

But while the other two had paused, both Alley Cat and Jackson instinctively launched from the bed – Jackson turning to shadow and hurtling to slam the door closed behind Jocelyn, while Alley Cat sprang for the mantel. She had seized and smashed the glass jug in an instant, and whirled toward the two women with a jagged shard of glass held like a knife.

Shrieking, both Jocelyn and Anika tripped into each other in their haste to retreat, and turned to shadow and mist in an effort to avoid being cut.

The last thing Jackson saw was the two women pushing at each other and scrabbling against each other in fear as their solid features evaporated. And then there was an odd moment of suspense while Jocelyn's shadow form jostled with Anika's mist form, as if they were tangled.

"What in the world?" Alley Cat asked, dropping her makeshift knife and putting her hands on her bare hips to frown at the twisting, frantic cloud that was forming between her and Jackson. "Have you ever seen this before?"

Jackson just shook his head in surprise, crossing his arms.

Slowly the churning shadows and mist were mixing into each other and disappearing. Soon there was nothing left in the dim red light but the prickling sparks that dance before a dizzy person's eyes – like a vision of bursting, tiny fireworks.

"Jocelyn?" Jackson asked tentatively. "Jocelyn come back or it'll be the end of Edward."

Alley Cat shook her head, but then, as if she had blinked, suddenly one surprised woman was standing where two had disappeared.

"Jocelyn?" Jackson asked again, uncertain.

"Or Anika," Alley Cat warned. But the woman was wearing what Jocelyn had worn.

"Neither, I think," the woman answered. "Or both." Her shoulders sagged and she touched the back of her hand to her brow, shaken deeply.

Jackson whistled in amazement. "Both," he told her. "I can feel it. You're new. You're whole. Balanced."

"All that matters is if she's an ally or not," Alley Cat stated bluntly.

"Oh I feel nothing overly dark or light about her," Jackson answered. "Just something oddly right. She probably has no real side." He regarded the woman again. "But I'll still be calling you Jocelyn."

She nodded, still dumbfounded. "I think I feel like I'm more Jocelyn than I've ever been," she told them shakily. "But I didn't really snuff out Anika like they feared. I just embraced her."

She blinked then, as if truly taking in the two naked people standing on either side of her.

"Though not quite like you were embracing each other."

Jackson scooped up his trousers and Alley Cat sighed, eyeing and then stepping back into her cat suit with distaste.

"So the fake image, which was to scare Mister White into hunting me down and bringing me in, was actually a stroke of genius," Jackson speculated. "We can become one again."

"It was fake? And to what end would we be joining for?" Jocelyn swallowed nervously. "What am I now? What is my purpose?"

"And how does it help us?" Alley Cat shrugged.

"Let's leave my little torture chamber and work it out on the go," Jackson suggested, smoothing his collar and opening the door. "We need to get ourselves into a strategic meeting place for Edward and The Curator."

"They're coming? How?" Jocelyn asked while Alley Cat checked the hallway and swiftly led their exit.

"I'm a living tracker," Jackson grinned. "They're drawn to me like moths to a flame."

"Anika!" Marilyn's voice echoed shrilly as the lightling turned into the corridor ahead of them. "What are you doing?!"

Two black eyed, corrupted goons rushed to flank Marilyn as they heard the alarm in her voice, and Jackson steeled himself for another near death experience. But, without batting an eye, Jocelyn disappeared and reappeared in front of Marilyn, shoving the lightling so that she flew backward to crash violently against the wall.

Marilyn was out cold and her goons were still blinking at the swirls of light in their vision while Jocelyn thrust a hand against both of their chests.

Immediately the tension and bravado left their postures as they relaxed against her touch. The darkness faded from their eyes and the softness of human feeling touched their faces.

"Sign yourselves out for the day, and don't come back," Jocelyn told them. And they nodded at this authoritative version of Anika Sweet. They turned together and hurried away.

"That's interesting," Jackson commented with interest.

"What did she do?" Alley Cat questioned, tugging him along again.

"They just became the two most beautifully balanced people to have ever lived," he answered. "I guess it's up to them which way they'll swing now. If they even will swing more toward dark or light at all."

"Yes," Jocelyn agreed with raised eyebrows as Alley Cat and Jackson joined her. "I think I've found my new purpose. And I feel stronger than ever."

"You sure showed Marilyn," Alley Cat agreed. "She had no chance."

"What'll we call you?" Jackson asked, alight with good cheer as they followed Alley Cat. "A neutraliser? The balancer? A leveller? Or madam sparkle-swirls?"

"We need to get into an ops-room that can be contained so you can contact Edward," Alley Cat cut in – hurrying through the maze of hallways as her eyes darted about sharply.

"He's already on his way," Jackson reminded her.

"But we want him to stop at the National Museum first," Alley Cat smiled. "Where you left his twin."

| 27 |

Advance

"You're sure?" Edward asked, gripping his phone tightly.

"I did it Edward," Jocelyn's voice soothed him. "You have to join with Marcus before you come here, or they'll be able to use their goons against you."

"But he's so oily," Edward grumbled, giving in.

"They're still good deep down," Jocelyn had the sound of a smile in her voice, and Edward smiled too – relieved.

"Absorb his essence into yours and it'll become new again," she went on. "You'll probably feel like the more dominant of the two of you, but ultimately, you'll have a mix of both of you in one."

"Oily and charming," Edward sighed. He glanced up at where Charlotte was draped across The Curator's lap, her arms around the dignified gentleman's neck while she crooned to him about her journey.

She had contacted Edward upon her return and had come at once to meet them. She had walked straight in, spotted The Curator, sized him up, and flopped herself across his legs in her state of 'utter exhaustion'. The bulky, usually stern man in turn appeared completely gratified by the liberties she had taken, and was listening avidly.

"Tell Jackson that Charlotte made it back, and we've got her with us," Edward informed Jocelyn. "She now has direct contact with almost every darkling in the world, if we ever need an urgent way to do so."

"I warned you that the lightlings can track communications," Edward heard Jackson's more distant voice.

"But Charlotte gave every darkling she made contact with a key to a new code that she made up," Edward answered. "It's brilliant. The lightlings might trace the location of the message recipients or senders, but they won't have a clue what the messages say. And it is only for emergencies."

"Brilliant," The Curator affirmed solemnly in the background. "Like a mix of Morse Code and verbal passwords."

"Oh it was just going back to old style coding," Charlotte told him humbly. "Pre-encryption days." She stroked her manicured fingernails down the nape of his neck.

"So the plan is to absorb Marcus Knight into myself before I come to CARE," Edward summed up. "But then what?"

"While you're doing that, get The Curator to track down the whereabouts of as many lightlings as he can," Alley Cat's voice simmered over the speaker then. "Charlotte can pass that information on to each darkling, and they can have fun hunting down and working out ways to force their lightling counterparts into joining before word spreads about what's going on. But get Charlotte to send out the warning that a lightling should not be approached while people are around

– or they'll just turn those people into thugs that a darkling can't beat."

"Right," Edward agreed, and he was glad to see that Charlotte and The Curator were managing to listen. "Spread the word," Edward recounted. "There needs to be a mass of joinings, but only when lightlings are alone and in mist form. Before lightlings become aware of the threat."

"We'll make a great team," Charlotte stroked The Curator's cheek appreciatively.

"Once you've spread the word you'll have to follow Edward to CARE, Charlotte," Jackson told her. "Marilyn is here, and so are some of the others."

"Alright. Hang in there," Edward told Jackson and the others. "I'll sort out Marcus and then wait until any other darklings who can find their counterpart in CARE can meet us. Then, as trusty Mister Knight, I'll lead them in."

"Good luck with your oily interactions," Jackson called. And then the call was disconnected.

"I'll come with you to the National Museum," Tiger told Edward, throwing a look of discomfort at Charlotte and The Curator. "And let them do their thing."

"We'll let the darklings who have counterparts in CARE's base know first," Charlotte said contentedly. "And we'll let the others know where they can find their own twins worldwide. Then we'll do our thing," she promised wickedly.

"We can trace lightlings by hacking into CARE employee records," The Curator told her, wheeling them both across to his centre screen so that she giggled. "It shouldn't be too hard now that Alley Cat is back in."

"Now who's brilliant?" Charlotte smiled coyly.

"Please let's go to the oily experience," Tiger grimaced, and Edward grinned, grabbing Tiger's arm and turning them both shadow even as they were stepping toward the door.

When they solidified again it was in the darkened rooms of The Curator's office gallery at the heart of the National Museum.

Tiger fetched The Curator's controller, and turned the lights of the expansive office on, but he didn't retract any of the protective seals yet.

"Is he behind there?" Tiger asked, gesturing with his chin toward an oddly rounded corner of the room.

Edward nodded, crossing to the painted screen. "Rush job," he shrugged, rubbing at some of the thinly spread, cracking paint so that they could peer into the chamber.

"Oh, yuck man," Tiger winced in disgust. "Surely that guy is dead."

"He has been," Edward agreed. "On and off for the last few days. But he's nearing death again now."

"So ... that's what repeatedly dying of asphyxiation looks like," Tiger swallowed sickly. "Red and purple and bulging and veiny. Oh, and bloated."

"I can't say I want that in me," Edward answered flatly. "But Jocelyn did it. So shall I."

"Alright, friend," Tiger shrugged. "How do you want to do this?"

Edward rolled his shoulders and straightened up. "Open it just a crack. He's too far gone to have heard any of this or to be thinking straight. But with a sliver of oxygen he'll revive enough to go back to instincts. He'll turn to mist to slither out of there and I'll be waiting."

"As you wish," Tiger answered. And when Edward had turned to shadow, he pressed the button for the seal to inch upward.

| 28 |

Revolution

"You can't stay locked in there forever," Mister White told them, his calm face filling the communications screen by the door. The shapes of many corrupted henchmen flanked him in the background.

"Well so far you haven't managed to un-hack your own evil ops room," Jackson smiled nicely. "So at least for now we can get comfy."

"Don't you usually think more long term?" Mister White questioned just as pleasantly. "And I only really want you. So you can slip out and leave the other two safely tucked away."

"It's good to feel wanted," Jackson mused. "But I know you really did want more than just me." He grinned darkly, coming to stand behind Alley Cat and pulling her to himself. He slid a finger under the lining of her cat suit's shoulder, pushing it down so he could kiss her skin.

Obligingly, she tilted her neck so that he could let his lips roam further.

"Your inappropriate displays are just time wasters to postpone the inevitable," Mister White replied more coolly, and Alley Cat felt the upward quirk and warmth as Jackson chuckled against her skin.

"Now I know there's some goody-two-shoes left in you," Jackson returned. "If you think this is inappropriate." He rubbed a hand down Alley Cat's hip and played with the high cut leg line of the cat suit. "You should have been there to witness the scene that Jocelyn was confronted with in our little torture room. That was practically pornographic."

"That little torture room was to be your own chambers in our great organisation," Mister White glowered. "You were to have a position of comfort. But I've come to wonder if my energies would be better spent on simply destroying rather than converting you."

"You would hurt your own flesh and blood?" Jackson gasped, resting his face against Alley Cat's cheek in sadness.

"Yes," Mister White answered simply. "Roll in the gas," he ordered.

At once a couple of his background followers began unwelding steel ventilation covers in the walls so that they could get into the shafts surrounding the sealed room.

"Anything you do will kill Alley Cat for good," Jackson warned more sharply, no longer stroking her skin but holding her in a more defensive way.

"I told you to come out," Mister White answered. "Alexis' loss will, again, be regrettable. But perhaps safest."

"You won't find out what I did to cure Alley Cat, or what happened to Anika," Jackson spoke more quickly.

"She'll turn up somewhere," Mister White smiled, and

nodded for two of his followers to slide their way into the walls.

"No she won't," Jocelyn cut in then. "You won't find her anywhere else."

"Don't," Alley Cat murmured. "Charlotte hasn't had enough time. They can't know."

"Pleading for your life, sweet pea?" Mister White drew closer to the screen.

There was a commotion behind Mister White then as Marilyn – dishevelled and bruised – pushed her way harshly through the milling black eyed guards.

"Anika is nowhere to be found, and they've done something to Jocelyn," Marilyn hissed. "She's stronger. Perhaps the experiments had some unexpected effects –" Marilyn paused when she caught sight of herself in the window open on the com-screen. She smoothed her hair and wiped at her smudged lipstick. "And we've had alerts go up in our branches world-wide. Lightlings are setting off their panic buttons – and are going missing."

"Stop!" Mister White ordered, and the shuffling sounds that had been getting closer in the walls around Jackson, Alley Cat and Jocelyn suddenly paused.

"Care to explain?" Mister White asked them.

"We're innocent. We've been locked in here," Jackson sighed. "Fearing for our lives."

"Very well," Mister White frowned. "Continue fearing. When two of the three of you are reborn we'll get the truth."

The scrabbling noises in the walls resumed, and there was the sound of drilling. Within moments four grill covers along their ops-room walls were dropping to the floor while canisters were thrown in like grenades.

"Toxic," Alley Cat winced, covering her nose and closing her eyes.

There was a picture of lungs on the nearest canister and the name of the product was 'SHREDDER'.

Jackson whirled Alley Cat into himself and held her face against his chest. "Jocelyn, this'll sting but our time wasting is up," he said as dark green fumes seeped quickly from the canisters. "Alley Cat keep holding your breath."

He turned to shadow, wrapping his essence around Alley Cat's like a blanket. Jocelyn followed suit and they rapidly sped through the nearest ventilation shafts, forced to follow the same exit route as those that had poisoned their air in the first place. There were no other quick openings to escape through.

The acidic fumes stung Jackson's already fragile being, as if electric currents were rolling through his essence, but he knew that he had at least covered Alley Cat.

"You joined us," Mister White announced as they hurtled free into the corridor.

At once Jackson saw that the passage had been cut off by an automated security door, and everywhere there were black eyed, corrupted humans.

In resignation he pulled up short and reappeared, holding Alley Cat steady as she drew in a gasp of air. Jocelyn appeared in a haze of swirling tricks of light, and Mister White paused for a moment in uncertainty. But then Jocelyn jerked as Marilyn leapt at her vengefully, and Mister White refocused.

Jackson pulled Alley Cat behind himself as Mister White stepped forward with a wolfish smile.

"I promise not to turn her again if you give yourself up," the lightling vouched graciously.

"I'll try to protect your back," Alley Cat muttered over Jackson's shoulder, and she lunged at two of the nearest black eyed recruits.

In a flurry of twists and thrusts she had knocked one out against a wall and she had stolen the baton off another. She twirled it experimentally before throwing herself back into the fight.

Marilyn was getting thrown around like a ragdoll by Jocelyn, and any other would-be attackers reeled back from her with sudden feelings of neutrality. But Mister White was intent on Jackson.

"Catch me if you can," he told Mister White, and began to evaporate – but a pair of female hands were suddenly around his neck, and the rolling, all-consuming build of darkness flowed from the corrupted woman's touch so that Jackson gasped and paused.

In that moment Mister White threw himself into Jackson – ramming him and his own female follower backward.

Jackson felt white hot agony as Mister White drove punch after punch into Jackson's already scorched ribs – along with overwhelming bursts of unrestrained goodness. At the same time the woman's darkness flooded Jackson's core – crashing against everything that Mister White was forcing into him.

Jackson groaned, collapsing between his two assailants with the woman beneath him and Mister White on top –

continuing to pound his twin to a pulp with fists that glowed white.

"This woman is a thirty-percenter," Mister White yelled as Jackson's eyes rolled, his body jolting with each shock of power. "And I'm just getting started."

"Jocelyn!" Alley Cat yelled, and Jackson felt Jocelyn's enhanced strength tearing the corrupted woman's arms from around his neck. The woman was yanked away to be nullified. But almost immediately two new corrupted men were in her place, as if this were the most desperate game of stacks on that had ever been played.

Jackson was hardly conscious when there was a dim yelp of surprise from Marilyn, and the sound of the automated security doors opening.

"Reinforcements," Mister White hissed in satisfaction, leaning in even harder on Jackson's chest.

Jackson screamed – feeling as if his very skin and all of his muscles were sizzling away from his blackening bones.

"Here!" Jackson heard Mister White growl with an effort. "Marcus, Marilyn, Anika, Jonathon – add your strength to mine!"

Jackson shuddered, recoiling from the thought of more goodness while his mind tripped on the overdose of dark waves crashing in from all other sides.

"Not Marcus," came Edward's voice.

"Not Marilyn," said Charlotte.

"I told you," added Jocelyn, "Anika's not here."

"And hey," came the last voice. "I'm Xander. There're a few others coming."

Jackson felt Mister White teeter as they all pulled him

backward and off of Jackson's chest, hauling the lightling up between themselves.

"Where are my lightlings?" Mister White panted, wide-eyed and stumped for a moment.

Jocelyn and Alley Cat pulled Jackson away from the grip of Mister White's corrupted men.

"He's in no shape to take on Mister White and come out as the dominant force," Jocelyn said worriedly. "His heart's ready to give out."

"Oh no it's not," Jackson groaned, limping free of them and grabbing the shirt fronts of the men they'd just detangled him from.

Wilfully, with abandon, he intentionally dragged every last drop of darkness from both of them – until he was ready to burst.

"Jackson!" Edward gaped, eyes wide as the darkness now whipped around his friend like a tangible being. "You'll die!"

"No," Jackson rasped. "He will."

And he threw himself at Mister White.

| 29 |

Saints and Sinners

He remembered Mister White had turned to mist – an act of panic and desperation to avoid Jackson's attack.

Then Jackson remembered turning to shadow and stabbing into his twin's essence like a spear. Their mingling forces had churned for what felt like an age. Not quite Jackson, and not quite Mister White anymore.

Both.

"At least we know we can still be reborn," Charlotte's voice broke through his consciousness.

"That was not just rebirth," Edward murmured. "That was resurrection."

"All that power that had been bottling between them made for a spectacular show," Jocelyn agreed.

Jackson frowned with his eyes still closed. "I'm ... always spectacular," he managed.

Charlotte's small hand touched his brow. "You are devilish, you are sweet, you are everything," she agreed.

"Why do I still feel like death then?" he asked, cracking his eyes open slightly. He was in Charlotte's bed. In the dungeon. Mick was lurking in the background like a hulking shadow.

"Well," Jocelyn mused. "We think you only just survived that one. You would have completely killed Mister White too with that level of darkness, if you hadn't taken him into yourself with all that goodness also in your veins. He really lost control of himself there."

"Right," Jackson winced, blinking up at them. "But I'm here. Am I still me?"

"Your pupils are all dilated, so you're probably still high," Charlotte answered matter-of-factly.

"More you than ever," Edward promised. "Maybe even more irresistibly magnetic than usual."

"As it should be," Jackson nodded.

"I think you actually created your own little miracle," Jocelyn told him. "You were the devil doing good and it saved your life. See, the ultimate type of goodness is when someone flawed and dark can still make the right decision, which you did. It made you both the darkest and best being in that circumstance. The strongest."

"Flawed?" Jackson joked, sitting up a little now. "Where are our people friends? You didn't let them die after all that did you?"

"Alley Cat and Tiger are coordinating a CARE re-structure. They'll be working for me," Charlotte informed Jackson gleefully. "I'm the queen of balanced judgment and neutrality now, so that's bad for business here. Mick's going to take over Charlotte's Bar."

"What is the world going to look like with you at its head …?" Jackson grimaced. "And no Charlotte in Charlotte's Bar."

"I'll still visit. And Sherice will be here. But I'll be working with The Curator to devise the best ways to undo the divisions that the lightlings created," Charlotte told him. "We'll be more like overseers and guides rather than world dictating masters until we work out what to do. Marilyn's memories tell me that we have a lot to do to sort out world-wide government systems in particular. Nothing will change without good governance in each country."

"Did … you grow up?" Jackson accepted a glass of water from Edward, still staring at Charlotte incredulously.

"Xander is leading lightling searches to catch any that were missed in our first effort," Jocelyn added. "It's trickier now that the lightlings know what's going on, so Edward and I plan to help."

"Leaving me alone again so soon," Jackson sighed.

"Just as you like it," Edward agreed. "But we're expecting you'll make more of an effort to check in on us as we sort out a whole new world."

"Especially me," Charlotte chimed in. "You won't be able to help yourself. You love to be in control."

"And to irk The Curator," Jackson nodded. "But I still feel odd," he admitted, rubbing at his chest disconcertedly.

Edward rose and offered Jackson a hand. "You've nearly had three true deaths in the last week. Nothing a shower and some liquor won't cure."

Jackson took Edward's hand and let his friend support him up from the bed. The others slipped away, but Edward stayed to help Jackson to the bathroom – Jackson's arm slung over the larger man's shoulders.

"Not to worry," Edward consoled. "We all felt odd at the

start. Like we were too big for our skins to hold." He helped Jackson to undress and switched the hot water on so that it ran down Jackson's spine in rivers.

"I feel too powerful for my own skin," Jackson admitted. "And that's while I'm weak as a lamb. What if I get stronger as I feel better and spontaneously combust?"

Edward grinned. "You definitely had more power to absorb and deal with, but we felt similar at first too. We've all dealt with it in our own ways. Charlotte has had The Curator to help her expend it all, and Mick too. I've had Jocelyn."

"Ah," Jackson grinned. "I see."

"And a night on the town is now more purposeful than just feeding our own dark cravings," Edward went on. "We have a job to do. We can make people healthier again. Wholesome. If we feel like they're struggling."

Jackson leaned his head back under the water for a moment. "But what does that make us? Rut fixers? Spiritual band aids?"

"We'll have to come up with a better name," Edward reassured him, leaning in to reach over Jackson and turn the water off. He handed Jackson a towel. "I'm sure you'll think of something to suit our new natures, just like you did last time, at the beginning."

"Huh," Jackson grunted.

Edward turned to leave him, but Jackson grabbed his belt and pulled him back, before turning the large man by his shoulders.

"Edward," he said slowly, holding his friend's deep brown gaze.

"Jackson?" Edward quirked an eyebrow.

Jackson squeezed Edward's massive shoulders. "I'm glad that this new beginning doesn't just have me alone in it this time."

Edward grinned. "As am I. But most of our kind will still be turning to you for answers."

"Which I won't have."

"But you will sound like you have them," Edward reassured him. "And then you'll do all you can to really have them."

"Just like last time," Jackson acquiesced, releasing Edward at last. "But maybe not tonight. I'll take a night off."

"You have a new black suit set out on Charlotte's chaise," Edward told him as he retreated from the room. "Figured it was too early for white."

Jackson rolled his eyes with a smirk, and when he was dry he dressed slowly, as if trying to reacquaint himself with his body.

He pushed his wet hair back to sweep away from his face, and clipped his cufflinks into place as he followed the staircase from Charlotte's room, up toward the growing thuds of pulsing, wild music.

"I'm glad you're awake Jax – Mister Flint," Sherice greeted him coyly as he emerged into the club. She was dressed like Eve in the Garden tonight, and he winked at her before testing himself – disappearing in a series of swirls to reappear – pressed between Jocelyn and Edward's dancing bodies.

He felt Jocelyn's arms circle around him from behind, and he reached back to drag her lips close – roughly kissing her and then leaning forward to bite Edward's neck. Then he disappeared again so that they could press back together.

Jackson reappeared in the shadows, seating himself to watch from an armchair away from the crowd.

A single gesture brought a mostly naked but very fluoro, body paint covered waiter to his side, brandishing a crystal glass with golden brandy ready.

Jackson shook his head as the man waited with hopeful, hungry eyes to see if there was anything else he could do. Disappointed, the man retreated to refill his tray at the bar, and Jackson noticed Tiger's wiry, tanned form leaning on the counter – relaxed and with his eyes on the crowd. Probably waiting for Charlotte and her Curator.

Jackson tilted his glass for a sip and felt the pleasant, heated sting of the alcohol on his tastebuds.

The fast, frenzied pace of the music seemed to quicken his own pulse so that it thudded with the beat.

Everywhere beyond his seat in the shadows there were bodies pressing together, moving to the sound as if they were animated by its power. Pushing in, rising and falling together in primal waves of dance.

He set his glass down, watching. Absorbing. But he felt slightly removed.

The dancers all blended together like always. Uninteresting.

Until he felt a stutter in his chest. An exciting lurch. When a brunette walked out of the thronging crowd with her dark eyes trained on him.

She wore grey, feathered angel wings with a lace choker at her throat, and she was the most interesting human being he had ever seen.

She walked in her weapon-like stilettos as if she owned the world, and gazed at him as if she owned him too.

Her face was illuminated in a flash of strobe lighting and was imprinted across his mind while everything else in the club became fragmented and dull. Silver, glittering eyeliner around her sharp eyes only heightened her strong features further.

A shining platinum bra hugged her chest and an excessively short skirt showed off her long legs as she stopped in front of him and leaned in, putting her hands on the armrests of his chair.

"Mind if I have this dance?" she brought her lips close to his ear.

Thrilling.

She took hold of his tie and drew him upward – his face inches from hers as they both straightened.

"I thought you and Tiger were working?" he asked over the music, putting his hands on the bare skin of her hips.

She smirked. "The new boss resides here." The words curled from her lips, and her highlighted eyes were keen and flashing in the lights. "But I noticed you. Alone and hiding in the shadows."

She pressed in, her perfume making his throat tingle.

"I work best from the shadows," he told her, reaching up to touch the pink curves of her lips.

"Not anymore," she disagreed, her arms around his neck as her body moved against his to the music – caressing and heating him all over.

She brushed her mouth against his, biting at his lip and

running her tongue lightly over the slight throb that she left him with.

Now it wasn't the music that was sending his pulse racing, or the alcohol that made his mouth burn.

He growled against her lips, his eyes dark with desire.

"Just a little longer in the shadows," he told her, and half blurring, half pushing her, he rammed her back against a wall. "With you."

She flicked open the drapes to a curtained room and dragged him in after her, throwing him onto a cushioned seat as if she owned the world, and as if he was worth everything in it.

She let him push the straps of the wings off her shoulders – dropping them to the floor.

He traced along the cups of her bra and then slid his fingers under the fabric.

"Take it off," he told her.

He slid his fingers under her skirt now, and hooked them in the waistline of her underwear.

"Take it all off," he whispered.

"Do you feel better?" she asked, keeping her eyes on him as she slowly unhooked her bra and then as she pushed her underwear down the length of her legs.

She leaned down to open his shirt and trace kisses over his chest.

"I feel much better," he promised, gripping her upper arms and throwing her down on the cushion littered rug on the floor. "All better."

Angled over her, he ran his fingers down her smooth stomach to the hem of her skirt. He pushed the hem up, settling it over her abdomen. Then he traced his way all the way down to the heat waiting for him between her legs.

Her eyes closed and her breasts pressed up against him as his fingers slid smoothly inside her.

His teeth pinched at her nipples and he made sure that his fingers were teasing at and priming her until he felt her muscles beginning to seize around his motions.

She gripped him desperately as he slowed and withdrew long enough to unzip his trousers and pull himself free. But she only left him free for as long as it took him to find a position that would allow him to keep stroking her in time to their thrusts.

He let his clothes disappear entirely – disintegrating away from him in a series of swirls and sparks. Then she closed in on him, and the music raged beyond them while the crescendo built within them.

She rubbed against his fingers and his length until the ecstatic cries that tore from their lips rang out as they clutched each other close – blind and wild with their passion.

When they collapsed in a sweaty, sated entanglement of limbs, all they could do was lie together amongst the cushions. Skin to skin, wrapped in each other and breathing hard.

It was some time before he drew his length out from between her legs and pulled her to lay across his chest, holding her in a one armed hug so that he could trace her breasts and trace the lazy smile on her lips with his fingertips.

"He's in there," a muffled, despondent voice came from the other side of the curtain. Sherice's voice.

"Jackson?" Charlotte said more clearly. "I need your advice –"

A strip of changing, multi-coloured lights flashed across Alley Cat and Jackson's exposed, embracing forms, and Charlotte stopped, suddenly smiling widely.

"Come back in a decade," Jackson told her, waving her away. "We're very busy."

"Of course," Charlotte agreed. "Have your fun now. And help me build the new world when you're done."

She flicked the curtain closed again.

Jackson tilted his head to peer down his nose at Alley Cat.

"Shall we take this back to your apartment, or my place?" he asked her.

"Why not both?" she asked in return.

He grinned. "Right you are," he said, pressing her to himself so that her breasts bulged against his chest. "I'm nowhere near done with you tonight."

And in a moment, they had turned to nothing more than a haze of twisting lights and swirls in the air.

Other books by Shelley Cass

'A Fairy's Tale' Epic Fantasy Series:
Book One – 'The Last Larnaeradee'
Book Two – 'The Raiden'
Book Three – 'The Army for the World'

Dystopian Future:
'Awaken Dreamer'

The Raze Warfare Series

The Sleep Sweet Series for children:
Book One – 'Little Pixie's Christmas'
Book Two – 'The case of the bored baby Ace'
Book Three – 'Mum and Me'
Book Four – 'The Cloud and the Flower'
Book Five – 'Hush'

Dear reader,
I would love to hear from you!
Please leave a review and feel free to visit my author
Facebook page or website (shelleycass.com).